Hprotecting the Heiress

ROYAL ELITE, BOOK ONE

To Sarah,
Stay chulzy!

NANA MALONE

Protecting the Heiress, Book 1 in The Heiress Duet
COPYRIGHT © 2019 by Nana Malone

Cover Art by Hang Le
Photography by Wander Aguilar
Edited by Angie Ramey, and Michele Ficht
Published in the United States of America

Protecting the Heiress

Chapter one

ARIEL

I was going to kill Roone if he'd sent me on a wild goose chase. I needed a team, and I'd take any help I could get in building one. But I had my doubts.

Jax Reynolds was my best lead, and so far, I'd found him… lacking. I'd been watching him for a month. So far all he had done was drink, skulk around, and pretend to be some kind of investigator-bodyguard type of person. How was this guy supposed to help me?

Do you really have a choice?

No. I didn't. Besides, Roone would never steer me wrong. Maybe he knew something about this guy that I didn't.

In the month I'd watched Jax, he'd been tracking someone called Max Teller. From what I'd seen, Teller had been a very bad boy. At least I knew from watching Jax that he didn't suck at tailing people.

I also knew he drank too much. It was one thing to be undercover, but he was taking undercover work to new heights. Max Teller had been at the pub Porkbelly every night. Which meant Jax had been there too. But instead of just sitting down and watching the guy, quietly skulking in a corner like every other normal PI, he posted up at the bar and slammed drink after drink.

I rolled my eyes. What had I gotten myself into?

You have no choice. Make your move.

The fall from Royal Guard grace had been a steep one.

Doesn't that apply to you, too?

Indeed, it did. But I had backing to start my own shop, thanks to King Sebastian, his wife and my bestie, Penny, and Roone my former partner and soon-to-be brother-in-law to the king. Basically, everyone I ever loved had put in all kinds of support, friend equity, and contacts. I refused to take their money. I had money saved up from working with the guard so long. I hadn't had to spend much of it and I'd made good investments, so I had enough to invest in the perfect location.

And before I could even blink, I had a roster of dozens of clients clamoring for my services. Some were easy enough that I could take care of them myself, basic network security kinds of things. I could manage all those clients. But also on that list waiting for me were clients that required actual physical presence, which meant I needed to hire some help quickly.

And Jax Reynolds was at the top of my list. Also on that list were Zia Barnes, a referral from Ethan, Tamsin Jacobs, a referral from Lucas, and Trace Lawson, a referral from my bestie. I had already interviewed Jameson Rhodes. She'd been new to the guard three years ago, but then she'd quit suddenly. With six of us on board, I could get started. Most jobs didn't require around-the-clock service, so I would be fine starting there.

I just prayed to God I didn't let everyone down. When I'd joined the Royal Guard, I never imagined that I would have to leave. That the palace would no longer be my home. But thanks to dear old dad, it wasn't my home, not anymore. So I had to make the best of it, which meant getting my ass in gear.

I followed Jax out of the pub. The guy he was tailing was some public-school-educated guy with money running out of his nose. From my quick look under the hood, Maxwell Teller had been a naughty boy, stealing corporate secrets. The company had hired Jax to get the proof and catch Teller in the act. I didn't know why they didn't just fire him after they suspected him, but there might be more to it than I knew.

Chiswick at night was still quite pretty in the main part of the village. But as I drove away from the high street, it became more industrial. Warehouses, dark alleys, chain-link fences. Signs that practically screamed *Keep the fuck out, dodgy as hell in here.*

Sure enough, Teller walked right on into dodge city. And Jax wasn't far behind him, which meant it was time to double-check my weapons. I zipped up my leather jacket, pulled up the hoodie attachment to cover my hair, and kept to the shadows.

From behind a dumpster, I watched as Reynolds made his approach on Teller, who was talking to someone else. I couldn't hear everything they were saying, but there was an exchange of words. And Jax's tone said everything. Pure sarcasm, derision. He loathed him. Or maybe it wasn't personal, and that was just how he talked.

There was a minor scuffle, and the man talking to Teller tried to run. When that didn't pan out, he attempted to hit Jax, which really didn't work out. Next thing I knew, Jax had the guy patted down and tied to a chain-link fence.

Teller tried to run, but Jax grabbed hold of him by the shirt collar before he could get too far. Teller struggled in his grip, and

I could hear Jax muttering something to him, his tone low and menacing. And then Jax had him in a head lock.

It took a few seconds, but Teller ran out of air and down he went. Jax's voice was a low murmur as he muttered, "Now, stay down, you arsehole." He was patting down Teller when trouble showed its face.

Another man had been hiding in the shadows, and he had the barrel of his gun pressed against Jax's neck.

I cursed under my breath. What? He didn't check to see if Teller had any friends or if the guy Teller was meeting came with anyone? Rookie mistake.

"Roone, are you sure about this guy?" I muttered to myself. Either way, I couldn't let him get shot in the back of the head. I made my calculations on what it would take to disarm the new guy while the barrel of his gun was at Jax's neck. Slowly, I approached, staying in the shadows. Surprise would have to work for me, and I hoped Jax was good at talking himself out of shit. I couldn't lose my new team member before he was *actually* even on my team.

My heart hammered in my chest as I watched Jax turn slowly, and he was talking. I could hear him better now. "What's the matter? Performance anxiety? You don't want to do it now?"

What the hell was he doing?

The assailant muttered something under his breath that I couldn't hear. And then I stepped out of the shadows, my own gun at the shorter man's neck. I whipped my hoodie off. "Tsk, tsk. Don't you boys know how to play nice?"

Jax's gaze flickered to me and then back to the guy between us. "Thanks for the assist, Red, but I'm good."

"Oh, yeah? You call this good? He was about to blow your head off."

"I promise, Red, I had it completely under control."

"Oh, sure you did."

The guy between us whipped his head back and forth. "Oi, if you two wankers can stop bickering, that would be great."

"Oh, you're in a hurry for me to shoot you?" I asked.

Jax chuckled. "I advise you to put your hands behind your back, let the pretty lady zip tie you, and wait patiently for the nick. I get the impression Red's handling some heavy weaponry there. She shoots, and you're going to get blood all over my nice jacket. And I love this jacket."

I glowered at him. "You'll have to do the zip-tying, if you don't mind."

He rolled his eyes. "Sure, sure, leave me to do all the work."

"You know what? Next time, I'll let the guy blow your head off."

Jax flashed a grin at me, and I could tell that, like Roone, he had that charming, roguish kind of swagger that women probably loved. Just not *this* woman. "You know, I'm still waiting for you to say thank you."

Jax zip-tied the guy and then secured him to a nearby pole. He slapped the guy on the cheek and grinned. "Don't move."

Then he turned his attention back to me. "Thank you. Now, do you mind me asking who the fuck you are?"

"I'm Ariel Scott. Roone Ainsley sent me. He's under the impression we could help each other."

Jax's brows lifted, and his gaze swept over me. I could see it, even in the dark. Mild interest. Curiosity. The hint of attraction. "Red, if you wanted a date, you probably should have approached me at the pub. But instead you tailed me over here and interrupted my business."

"Please, you were so busy drinking at the bar you didn't even see me."

"Oh, you've been on my tail for at least two weeks. Of

course I saw you."

"No way you saw me. You're making some educated guesses right now. And P.S., you shouldn't drink on a job."

"Ginger ale, love. You think I don't know any better?"

"God, I will kill Roone. Why did he send me to you?"

"I don't know, love. But whatever his reason, it's not happening. I don't need any help."

"Are you insane? Your life is in the shitter."

"Huh, says the redhead skulking in the shadows. Something tells me if you're looking for me to help you, your life's not much better off than mine."

He had a point there. "Roone said we could help each other, so I'm here."

"Yeah, Roone, good mate. But even good mates make mistakes. I'm not interested in whatever you're selling." He brushed past me.

"Where are you going?"

He dug through the pockets of Max Teller, who was coming to and moaning. Jax fished out a flash drive then muttered, "Thanks, Max. Pleasure doing business with you. Do try and stay out of trouble now, won't you?" Then he stood and headed back toward the alley exit.

"Wait. You haven't even heard my proposal."

"I don't need to hear it. I'm not interested."

What the hell? I followed after him. "You haven't even heard it yet. And, let's face it, you owe me now."

"No, I don't owe you. I didn't ask you to follow me. Like I said, you're not that good at it."

"Oh, I'm excellent at it."

He laughed. "I've seen you at the pub every day this week. Your hair. Either cover it or dye it. I saw you outside my flat too."

"Oh, really? Just at the pub and outside your flat? Where else did you see me?"

His brows furrowed. "Does it matter?"

I grinned. "Oh, you didn't see me everywhere. Interesting."

"Where else were you?" He crossed his arms.

"Teller's office. I was one of the security guards. I also managed to get in as a day temp. I guess you missed that one. I knew you were tailing him, so I figured it'd be easier to tail you if I could get in closer to Teller."

He lifted one brow then and assessed me more shrewdly. "What day?"

I shrugged. "Tuesday last week."

"I knew it. I saw you at the sandwich cart."

I grinned at him. "Yeah, but you didn't *recognize* me, did you?"

"You looked familiar."

"Did I? Or did you just want to bang me? Don't think I didn't notice you staring at my ass."

He shrugged. "I'm a bloke. I'm born to look. Besides, redheads aren't my type."

"That's okay. Overbearing roguish assholes aren't my type either. But I need your help, and you're going to give it to me."

He chuckled low, and the sound was rich, deep, and mellow. "Oh yeah? What makes you say that?"

"Because if you help me, I can get you the one thing that you want."

The glower turned more into a sneer then. "You don't know what I want."

"Oh, but I do. You want back in the Royal Guard. And I can give that to you."

Chapter *Two*

JAX

The banging at my front door was incessant. I had woken up early as always, but I'd been too knackered to bother to get out of bed. What the fuck had happened last night?

First that little shit had gotten the drop on me. Then I'd been saved by the crazy redhead. The crazy, persistent redhead who was banging on my front door at the moment.

There she was in my camera's view, knocking away. She was cute. Irritating. Bossy. And *determined*.

I sat up and glared at my clock. Six-bloody-thirty a.m. Apparently, she was also a goddam pain in the ass.

After I'd relieved Teller of the flash drive in the alley, she'd followed me all the way back to my car, insistent that we were going to talk. She laid out her options. Me, coming back to the Winston Isles, working for her, helping her start her business.

And then in a year's time she said she could get me back in the Royal Guard.

That was the goal. It was the only thing that mattered. Getting back to the Royal Guard.

Yeah, well, didn't you throw it away?

Yes, I had. I'd thought that Kyla was the one. She'd told me how much she wanted to have a family with me, and that was everything I'd ever wanted in my life. The family, the ruckus, the house with lots of kids running around everywhere. The life I'd had growing up.

When she got pregnant, she wanted me to leave the Guard. She said it was too dangerous and that she would rather I do something that didn't involve carrying a gun or potentially getting shot at.

I'd done what she asked. Of course, six months later, I'd found out the baby wasn't mine and that she'd been having an affair with her boss, the cross-eyed twat.

I'd given up everything for her. So I was back in London, doing a job I liked but that was hardly fulfilling. All because I'd made a misstep. And once you were out of the Guard, you were out of the Guard for good.

Or was I?

She shifted on her feet impatiently. "I know you're watching me. You think I can't see the camera? Open the door."

"Jesus fucking Christ," I muttered to myself as I shoved off the covers. It was still cold enough to make me grab a long-sleeve jumper off my dresser before heading downstairs to the door. When I yanked open the door, I glowered down at her. "Woman, do you know what time it is?"

"I happen to know that you wake up at five a.m. like clockwork. We're losing time."

I rolled my eyes. She didn't seem to care. She barged right by me and started stomping up my stairs. "Where's the kitchen?"

"Come right in, why don't you?"

"I need coffee, and then I can be more chipper."

"Sweetheart, I'm not sure I want to see you chipper."

She flipped me off and made a right toward my kitchen, finding it easily in the loft-like space. But when she opened my cupboards, she groaned. "Oh, what is wrong with you Brits and your fucking tea?"

I leisurely strolled into the kitchen and grinned as I leaned against the cupboard. "Well, if you weren't so rude, I would tell you where I've stashed some coffee."

She whirled around, red hair flying over her shoulders. "Oh my god, I'll do anything for coffee. I swear. I might even leave you alone for a couple of hours."

I rolled my eyes and reached above her to the top shelf where, even though she was tallish, she probably couldn't see. I pulled down some coffee pods and the coffee maker that Kyla had insisted on.

I plugged it in then quickly set it up for her before shoving in one of the pods. "Coffee. Now will you go away?"

"Sorry, I lied."

"Well, you don't say."

"Look, I wouldn't be all up your ass—"

"Careful sweetheart, I might like it like that."

A smirk lit her lips. "Hey, I don't judge. I need your help."

"You have a funny way of asking for it."

As the coffee brewed, I could see her practically dancing from foot to foot. She was a grade-A caffeine addict. *Noted.*

"What is it about my proposition that you don't like?"

"You mean besides the part about returning to the Winston Isles?"

"Everything in your file said you were a Royal Guard with

distinction. You have friends. You have a network. Why wouldn't you go back?"

Good question. Why wouldn't you?

After my parents' death, the Guard had been the only family I'd known. I knew it would hurt to see them on the island, still a unit that I wasn't part of and that I would never be part of again. "It's private."

"No. No, it's not. I have your files. I've seen it all. You were good at your job. And then you just packed up and left. And what, now you're a PI? I mean the flat's nice, but can that be really satisfying?"

I shrugged. "It's like sex. Even if it's bad, at least you're still having sex."

She rolled her eyes. When the coffee was done, she pulled her mug out and took a sip. No sugar no cream. Just straight black.

Okay then.

"Why me? Why are you here?"

"Because as annoying as he is, I trust Roone. Your name is the first one he gave me. He said I could count on you to watch my back and that you were looking for a chance back into the Guard. I can give you that chance. Why would you say no?"

"You don't know me. I don't know you. I don't make it a habit of jumping into bed with people I don't know."

She sputtered then, spraying coffee everywhere. "I beg to differ. Three weeks ago, you pulled some blonde out of a bar for—"

I scowled at her. "Never you mind that."

"Well you're the one who said—"

Jesus. She really had been tailing me for that long, and I hadn't noticed? I cleared my throat. "Look. I appreciate the reference from Roone. He's a good mate. But I'm not going back."

She took another, more measured, sip of her coffee this time. "Oh, you're coming back." She reached in her back pocket and plunked down a ticket. "That's for you. We leave tomorrow."

I laughed then. "Sure of yourself, aren't you?"

She glanced around at my sparse surroundings. I liked my flat. It was nondescript. Quiet. My neighbors didn't bother me. I could come and go as I pleased.

But there was nothing personal there. No hint of a *real* life.

"Oh, something tells me you're coming." She took another long sip and placed her mug down. "I'd offer to clean up, but it's not really my thing. I'll see you tomorrow. I've got to gather the rest of the team, and I'll need your help with background checks."

"Love—"

"Ariel."

I rolled my eyes. "Really? With the red hair? The mermaid reference?"

Her shoulders went stiff. "Yeah, my father's idea. Whatever."

I shrugged. "Look, *Ariel*, nice to meet you and all, but the answer is no."

She grinned at me then. That smile softened all her hard edges. It made her incredibly striking, and I wondered what it would be like if she actually laughed.

"I mean it. The answer is no."

"You know, you're not the first guy to tell me no. You probably won't be the last. I'll see you tomorrow morning. It's a private jet. At least go back to the island in style."

And with that, she sauntered back down the stairs. I could hear the front door snick shut as she skipped out.

My gaze flickered to the ticket on the table. Going back

would mean everyone would know I'd failed. Going back would mean I had no family. Not the one I'd left for, and not the one I'd left. It still burned a hole in my chest knowing how badly I'd fucked up.

It's not like you have family here anyway.

All my brothers and sisters were scattered around the world. We'd all grown up on the islands. My two eldest sisters had moved back to the UK, but one lived in Scotland, and the other lived in the West Midlands. No one was in London. Seeing them was relatively easy, just a train ride away. But still, it wasn't the same as coming home to family.

My brothers were scattered as well. Two in Australia and one in the States. And then my baby sister, she was in South Africa. So I had no one left in the islands since our parents were gone, which meant the Guard was my only family.

Except, not anymore.

Could I face them? Could I handle knowing I wasn't part of them anymore?

But if she's telling the truth …

If she was telling the truth, this was my shot. My way back. A way around the rules. But who was this Ariel? Could she be trusted?

Remember what happened the last time you trusted a woman.

Yeah, a woman that promised me everything. At the same time, the ticket sat there calling my name. Beckoning me.

It was a shot. A chance to correct the wrongs. A way back into the life I knew that I had always wanted.

I ran a hand through my hair and leaned my head back against the wall. That redhead was a pain in the ass, but she was also right. I was taking that ticket. She'd dangled a carrot I couldn't say no to. I just hoped my old mate Roone was right about the both of us.

NEELA

I will not key his car. I will not key his car. I will not key the dick's car.

I passed my ex boyfriend's shiny new BMW outside of the office we'd once shared, and I had to force myself to hold back. What the hell was he doing here?

Wasn't it enough that he'd dumped me and taken half our clients? He had to force me to see him every damn day this week? Why couldn't he slink back under a rock and let me pick up the scattered pieces of my life?

I left his car unscratched… mostly because a meter maid was patrolling the road and I didn't want a vandalism charge on top of everything else. So just like usual, the jackass robbed me of any kind of satisfaction.

Libido: *Ain't that the truth.*

When I walked in to my mostly empty office, I swallowed the pang of regret. I was in this mess because I'd made a mistake. Against my better judgment, I'd opened a business with my boyfriend. And now I would have to pull a rabbit out of the hat if I wanted to continue.

My assistant saw me and trotted over. "Mayday, mayday, asshole on premises."

"I know, Bex. I saw his car outside."

"He's in the file room. Adam is trying to stop him, but—"

I sighed. Was Richard always such an asshole? Had I just not seen it?

Survey says: Yes.

"You want I should key his car?" Bex asked hopefully?

"Nah. I already considered it, but there were too many witnesses."

She rolled her eyes and headed back to her desk to pick up the phone. I ran into Mr. Disappointment as he was coming out of the server room, my sole remaining cryptanalyst, Adam, hot on his heels.

Adam glowered at him as he marched him out.

Richard was not impressed. He'd never liked Adam. He'd always been jealous of him. More than once he'd tried to get me to fire him, even though he was our best cryptanalyst.

"I made sure he only took approved data, Neela."

"Thanks Adam, I've got it from here." When he was out of earshot, I scowled at Richard. "Are you seriously leaving me with no clients?"

The man I'd thought I loved shrugged, and I wondered how I'd ever found him so irresistible.

With the dishwater-blond hair and his light blue eyes, Richard had that look to him, clean cut, polished. And when he smiled, he seemed fun and youthful. But now he was stabbing me in the back with a fourteen-inch blade.

"It's not my fault the clients prefer me to you."

"You're not even a cryptanalyst. How do you plan to keep the clients you've siphoned away?"

He shrugged. "Your skills are a dime a dozen. Besides we split the company. Don't be bitter."

"You're full of shit, and you know that. These are clients *I* nurtured. Clients *I* built."

"Yeah, well, they're my clients now. You should be happy I left you with some."

I narrowed my gaze at him. "When did you become such an asshole?"

"I was never an asshole. I'm not being an asshole now. We started this business together. I should have known better than to mix business and pleasure. We both said we'd be adults about this."

No. No way he was twisting this on me. "Our agreement says that should we dissolve the company it would be an even split. How is it even when you've taken the biggest earning clients for yourself?"

"You act as if you don't have any clients, Neela. You were always too melodramatic. Why can't you just be..."

His gaze scanned over me. I could see it. His disappointment. *Asshole.* I'd sold myself short when I'd settled for him.

I could tell myself I'd been caught up in the fun of starting our own shop. Four years ago, fresh out of Uni, we'd both been employed at RAM Technologies. I was a junior cryptanalyst and he had been on the technical sales side. I'd told him about my love of puzzles and how my father had always had a dream of starting his own shop. Breaking out of the mold of academia. Doing something exciting. Richard had convinced me that we could do it together.

And we had. Now he was walking out the door with the fruits of my labor. I'd believed in him. Sure, he was leaving me half the clients. They just happened to be the half that wouldn't hit their revenue potential for years. I had a company to run.

The truth was I'd settled for him. I'd known better, but he'd been convenient and smart, and we had similar goals.

Oh yeah... sounds real hot and heavy.

And that was just it. There was nothing hot and heavy about any part of our relationship. But I'd hung in there like an idiot because there was more to life than excitement.

Then he broke up with me and dissolved our company, giving me more excitement than I ever hoped to have. "How am I supposed to keep the company running?"

He shrugged. "Not my problem. And remember, any massive revenue or asset you bring in during the next month is still subject to our fifty-fifty split for the next thirty days. They can be seen as assets to the company, and I deserve half."

"The hell you do." I would fight him tooth and nail. Basically, under the terms of the agreement, for the next thirty days I needed to make the clients I had work better. Any new business, he could take half of and vice versa.

The difference was he would survive the next month.

"So you've stripped me of everything I've got. And then during that crucial time when I need to be able to make changes to right my part of the ship, you take away my ability to do that."

"Yeah, well, it's called business. You're a competitor now."

"God, I hate you."

"No, you don't."

I'd never hated anyone before in my life. And maybe I didn't hate him. That was a strong word. A strong emotion. I usually thrived on keeping myself balanced. Wild emotions caused people to stop loving you when you had wild swings like that. I'd learned early not to react emotionally, and I needed to remember that now. "You know what. It's for the best. I don't need anything from you."

"Yeah, you do. I can't believe I wasted all my time with you."

I refused to wince no matter how much that one hurt. Emotional blackmail. But I was free now. "Get the hell out."

"Oh, I'm going. Just cleaning out the rest of my stuff."

As he carried his last box out, I glowered at him. Bex had already offered to kill him in his sleep on my behalf. I'd declined, but at the moment, it didn't sound like the worst idea.

I was honestly surprised that Adam stayed. He was the brightest of the ten cryptanalysts that we'd had. It would be a while until I could properly pay him. I knew Bex was staying because she was my best friend and she had always hated Richard. But honestly, if I was being fair, I should let them both go so that they could find paying jobs. I could always hire them back if and when I got some revenue-producing clients.

The front door swung open before Richard finished collecting his things, and a guy in a suit walked in. Slim, brown hair, kind eyes. But his suit was crumpled and looked to be wool. He must be sweltering. "Miss Wellbrook?"

"Yes?"

"I have a summons for you."

I frowned. "Oh, fantastic. What about?"

He shook his head. "I'm just the messenger."

I took it from him, and Richard paused at the door. "If it has to do with the business, you know that involves me too."

"Yes, well if it has to do with the business, I will notify you."

"Well, I'm here now, so why don't you tell me."

I scowled at him as I ripped open the summons. I could see Bex gripping something tightly at her desk. I had a feeling it was a pen or a letter opener or something. Adam, bless him, stood by the door, glaring at Richard.

My eyes quickly scanned the papers, and then my heart sank. My stomach flipped, and my knees weakened. The room spun. "Oh my god."

Bex was on me in a second. She dropped something on the floor, and I vaguely registered it was indeed a letter opener. Adam had a chair under my ass just in time before I sank. For a moment Richard hesitated at the door, looking almost concerned. Bex blocked him out though, thank god. "What? What is it?"

"It's Willa. She's gone."

My oldest friend. The only friend I'd had from childhood. She was dead. And from the looks of it, there was something she'd left me.

Chapter *Three*

NEELA

"I don't understand. What do you mean, she left me her baby?"

Mr. Bipps reached across his oak desk and patted my hand. "I know this must come as quite a shock. Not to worry. I'll walk you through everything."

A shock? More like a hiss of cold wind had found a crack in my armor and settled in, freezing everything so I couldn't possibly feel anything ever again. Except this wasn't the blissful numbing of a gray day. It was the cold bitter numbing that eventually brought you nothing but pain.

I'd known Willa was pregnant. But she was still living her party lifestyle. That was what our fight had been about. I never wanted to be judgy... Oh, who was I kidding? I'd totally judged her. But the late nights... The kinds of people she was hanging out with? I'd seen her drinking champagne at a benefit, and I'd suggested she needed to lay off for the sake of the baby.

She'd called me sanctimonious and boring then tried to suggest that wine was good for the baby. We'd said things to each other, things we couldn't take back.

Things you'll never be able to take back.

We hadn't spoken or seen each other since then. I'd never even met her daughter, Mayzie.

I rapidly blinked back the tears. "Is Mayzie..." My voice trailed. "Is she okay? Healthy? No complications?" At the time, I'd suspected that Willa had been doing other unhealthy things while pregnant, like taking party drugs. She'd dabbled before.

Mr. Bipps nodded emphatically. "Yes. Yes. Normal, healthy baby girl. She's now thirteen months old." He nodded as he adjusted the glasses on the end of his nose to read what looked like some medical charts.

He reminded me of someone's grandfather. Chalk-white hair sticking up at the edges, like he'd made some attempt to tame its unruly curls. But his hair had resisted any gel, which, considering we're in the islands, was entirely expected.

"I just—I can't believe she's gone." I'd pushed too hard for her to be responsible. I should have just loved her for her spirit. Classic Willa, she'd fought me.

"Ms. Wellbrook, I know this is quite the shock, but Mayzie is the most pressing issue. You were very specifically listed in Willa's will and trust. You are to have sole guardianship of Mayzie."

My stomach cramped. How in the world was I supposed to look after a baby? I'd just lost everything I'd spent the last several years building. My head spun with the dizzying reality.

You can always say no.

The hell I could.

I'd once been that kid left with no parents. Willa's parents had taken me in. Fed me, clothed me, looked after me.

And made sure you felt every single one of their sacrifices.

My mother had died when I was two. My dad when I was eight. He'd set up a trust for me, but it had really just been for college.

None of it made any sense. Willa MacKenzie and I had been best friends since we were little girls, but we'd been complete opposites in every way. For all my hyper responsibility, Willa was a free spirit. Always had been. I sometimes wondered if she had the right attitude about life, because while I worked my butt off to keep my company in the black, Willa lived in the lap of luxury as an art dealer.

She went to fabulous parties, rubbed elbows with celebrities, and had basically the kind of life that should make everyone jealous.

Except, I wasn't jealous. While that life suited Willa just fine, I wasn't interested in late nights, seeing and being seen at parties, or men so handsome I couldn't even look them in the eye. I liked the quieter life. But I could always count on Willa to bring the fun. She pulled me out of my shell and made me go on some crazy adventures, but the key was I got to come home from that. Not Willa, though.

"What about her father?"

"Not in the picture. He's not named on the birth certificate."

"That poor baby." I then asked the question I wanted to avoid. "What about Mrs.—" I stopped myself. I was an adult. I was no longer being forced to call her Mrs. MacKenzie. "What about Jane?"

"Miss MacKenzie was quite clear that her mother was not to have guardianship of Mayzie."

Oh god. This really was on me. I had no idea how the hell I was going to feed myself and this kid.

Do you really have a choice?

No. I didn't. Willa's daughter needed me. And I *would* do it differently. Not at all like the MacKenzies. I'd give her as much love as possible. I would never make her feel like an unwanted inconvenience.

The MacKenzies had taken me in, but from the start they'd made it clear that I was *not* actually part of the family. I'd had to call them Mr. and Mrs. MacKenzie, just like before my father died. When they went on vacation, I stayed with a friend of theirs. I always shared a birthday party with Willa, even though my birthday was three months prior, and I'd only get to invite one friend. It was fine, Willa was the friend I would have chosen, but still.

Those little digs and slights had made me more than eager to get out of the house. They'd even suggested that I needed to use my college savings to pay them back instead of going abroad to MIT. Luckily, my father's trust had been very specific.

I dragged my attention back to Mr. Bipps. "What happened exactly?"

"Seems like a car accident off the coast road heading up to the hills. It looks like she swerved to avoid something and couldn't correct. The car went right off the road and crashed into the water. They didn't recover a body, but the car was significantly mangled, and her blood was found in the vehicle."

I sucked in a sharp breath. Shit. This was real. Very, very real. It wasn't a nightmare I could wake up from. "Poor Willa."

He gave me a sympathetic nod. "There is more, Miss Wellbrook. Willa left the entirety of her estate to Mayzie. She named you as guardian and eventual trustee. In the first year following her death, I am to remain the trustee. After a year, that responsibility will shift to you. You will receive a monthly allowance that will cover everything needed to help you look after

Mayzie. Major financial and property decisions, I'll handle. But I'd very much like to include you, if you don't mind, so you can get a feel of what you'll need to do."

I blinked at him. "Excuse me?" My brain had barely registered the words *properties* and *estate* and *trustee*.

"Yes, properties. The House in Nob Hill. The flat on Winston Beach. And the rental property on Royal Row."

I blinked. "I—" My brain stuttered. I'd known Willa was doing well, but that well?

"She did, in fact, do quite well for herself."

A trust. So, Willa had apparently learned from my father's example. "I'm sorry. This is all so difficult to process."

"I understand. I'm here to help. There was something else she left to you." He stood and walked over to his wall safe, a slight limp noticeable in his gait. His knobbed hands twisted the dial. He was old school. I could respect that.

"What is it?"

He pulled open the safe then took out a leather-bound journal of sorts. "I believe it's a journal."

He handed it to me, and I was surprised how heavy it was. When I opened it, I frowned. "I don't understand." I flipped the pages, but they were filled with lines of symbols I didn't understand or recognize.

"In her notes, she said, 'Unlock it for me, Neela.'" He blinked up at me. "Do you know what that means?"

"I—" I stared at the symbols and willed my brain to engage, but nothing. I didn't recognize the symbols. "I'm a cryptanalyst. I unlock and create codes for a living. Maybe that's what she meant, but I have no frame of reference for this."

"Well, it seems she wanted you to figure out the code."

"I mean, maybe, but without knowing what it is, it'll be next to impossible."

"Yet, she left it to you."

"I guess she did." I slipped the journal into my bag as my mind tried to work out what the hell Willa had been up to.

"There is one more thing."

"Oh?"

He sat back and ran a hand through his too curly white hair, making it look even more crazed and making him resemble more of a mad scientist than a respected lawyer. "As you know, I'm her lawyer. And now that she's passed, I'm no longer bound by attorney-client privilege. You will be the eventual trustee of Mayzie's trust. Willa was extremely wealthy. How she got that wealth, while not quite *illegal*, occasionally meant questionable people were in her life."

What was he talking about?

"Questionable?"

He sighed. " Willa was very wealthy. And by extension, her daughter is very wealthy. I would suggest you hire security. There is already staff at the Cross Oak house in Nob Hill. But I would suggest someone you can personally vet. If you like, I can send you a list of options."

"Security? Like people who follow me around and stuff? That's insane. I'm sure a good security system at the house should be enough. I think you'll find I live a very different life-style than Willa did."

I had grown up with the kind of men he was talking about and I wanted none of it.

He nodded. "I understand. All the same, please, at least con-sider it. For Mayzie's sake. Her mother was constantly worried about security, and now Mayzie is a very wealthy little girl. The kidnap and ransom trade can be quite lucrative to some. You need to take precautions."

Precautions? Who the hell did Willa do business with? The

most I ever had to worry about was making sure my client was happy and figuring out if I should get a dog or not. I didn't travel like Willa did. Or rub shoulders with anyone even remotely interesting, let alone dangerous.

"I know you mean well. Really. But the kind of work my father did necessitated constant security. He did the kind of classified stuff governments don't even want their own people knowing about. It takes a toll on someone, living in that constant state of *something bad could happen*. I firmly believe that constant worry caused his heart attack. I think I'll see how we get on first. What I really will need assistance with is finding a nanny. I assume the monthly stipend will allow me to hire someone? I run my own business, and I think at least in the early days, I'll need to figure out how to juggle it all."

He sighed. "Of course. I'll approve that as separate from the stipend, though it will be more than substantial. I'll send you recommendations for that position as well."

Suddenly the weight of what I was agreeing to weighed on me, sitting on my chest like an anvil. "I don't know if I can do this."

He leaned forward then. "You can because you must. Mayzie needs you."

JAX

I was *home*. And to be honest, I wasn't sure yet how I felt about it. But it was a chance, just the chance that I needed, so I was going to take it.

And Red hadn't been lying. She had some seriously nice digs along Castle Road. Empty, but a good space. Big enough for a team. But at the moment, it was just the two of us. "So, where's everyone else?"

She turned and grinned at me. "Just get right to it, why don't you? We actually have a job. We're meeting the client later this morning. But after that I get on a plane to the States. I have a new teammate to go recruit."

"Are you going to bully them into joining this rag tag team, too?"

She lifted a delicately arched brow. "I didn't bully you. I just made you an offer you couldn't refuse. And just so we're clear, I will hold up my end of the bargain. You want back in the Guard, and I will do everything in my power to make sure that happens."

I gave her a brusque nod. With my duffle still slung over my shoulder, I angled my head up toward what looked like loft spaces. "Those the bedrooms up there?"

She nodded. "Yeah. It's a combo live-work space. I'll have some men in here doing some work to make it more comfortable. There are beds in the two corner rooms. One of those mine. You can have the other one. Since you're first, you can have the biggest room. I don't anticipate all of us will live here, but it's an option if needed. Beds are being delivered for the other rooms tomorrow. And each room has a private bathroom attached, so that's helpful."

"Looks like you thought of everything."

"No, not quite everything. But I'm getting there."

I watched as she shifted on her feet. She was antsy. Wanted to get to work. I recognized the look. It was how I was too. I dropped my duffle near the massive glass table in what looked like the communal conference space or dining area. "Why don't you tell me about the job. Then I'll get settled in, and you can take off to wherever it is you need to go."

The smile she gave me was sweet, but I knew better than to

be tempted by a sweet smile. "Thank God. I'm not great at small talk. Sort of direct and to the point. I didn't want this to be awkward, but I'd rather just get to work."

I chuckled. "So far it looks like we'll get along great."

She gave me a wry smile. "Sorry about haranguing you in London."

"You should be."

Her jaw fell open. "To be fair, I wasn't exactly *haranguing*. You knew you wanted to take the job. You were just playing hard to get."

I slid my gaze over her. I wasn't sure if she was flirting or not. Should I flirt back?

No dumbass. No matter what, she's your boss. And you've already had one messy situation.

I wasn't going there. "So, what's the job?"

"Bodyguard gig. Should be fairly simple and straightforward. I'm not sure how much coverage is needed, but it will likely be a two-man gig in shifts."

"Every day or for an event?"

"I know nothing. All I know is I got the referral call for us to go meet the client to check out their needs. A referral call is a referral call. There are some other gigs I have on the line, but that one seems the most pressing and promising."

I nodded. "Are you going to tell me something at least personal about you? So we're not strangers?"

"We're *not* strangers. I had to listen to you snore all the way on the flight across the pond. I know you mumble in your sleep and then laugh a little. And then you talk to yourself. Whatever it is you're saying to yourself, you seem self-satisfied because then you get this smug smile on your face."

I scowled at her. "I do not talk in my sleep, and I'm not smug."

"Okay, if you say so." She shrugged then. "What do you

want to know?"

"Well, obviously you were a Royal Guard. What happened?"

"Not that much of a story really. After helping secure the lost princess, it was time for me to go. You know, exacerbated by the fact that my father was tied up in the conspiracy."

I winced. "Mother fucker."

"Yeah. And that's really it. I chose to leave instead of being ousted by the Council."

"I'm sorry. Blimey, mate. Certainly not your choice."

"Nope. But Sebastian and Lucas, Penny, they've all been super supportive."

I lifted both brows. "You're on a first name basis with the king?"

"Yeah, uh, his wife Penny is my best friend."

"Oh, so that's how you're going to get me back in the Guard?"

"Doesn't matter how I'm going to do it, just that I do it, right?"

She had a point there. "Fair enough." I pointed around at the sparse but slick surroundings. "So, this. The king set you up?"

"No." She looked around with a faint hint of a smile floating over her lips. "This I did myself. I was in Guard housing, so I never had to pay for rent, and I was just saving it. I don't have expensive tastes or hobbies. All the money I've been saving over the years went into this place. It'll go into initial salaries. And we already have clients, so I'll be able to get us off the ground."

"You're serious about this. You're going to make this work."

"Why would you ever start anything if you weren't serious about it?"

Oh boy. I liked her already. She was still a pain in the ass, though. "So, what? You married? Boyfriend? Girlfriend? Asexual?

"Not married. No boyfriend *or* girlfriend. And I'm very

much sexual, but my entire focus is on the business right now. "

Good. She wasn't here to fuck around. Neither was I. We were going to get along fine.

"I want to make this place like home you know? I just left a team that I loved working with. They were a family. I'd like this team to feel the same way."

I shrugged. "Okay. How do you plan on doing that?"

"Well, first things first. No matter what, monthly Sunday dinners with the whole team."

I laughed. "What, like my mum used to make us do?"

"Yeah. Exactly like that. I think it'll help us all get to know each other quickly. And we'll get to figure out personalities. Think of it as a business meeting minus any talk about work."

"Whatever floats your boat." I'd do the jobs she needed me to do, and then I'd be back in the Royal Guard, so whatever flower-child, hippie way she had of running her business wouldn't affect me for too long. "That's fine, I guess."

"What about you? What's your story? All I know is that you left the guard nine months ago. Doesn't say why."

Something told me she already knew the reason but wanted me to tell her, and she wanted to suss out if I would tell her the truth or not. "I left because my girlfriend was pregnant. She didn't want me to have a job that involved me getting shot at on occasion, so I left." Maybe she would just stop there.

"And?"

That was too good to be true. "And we went to London only for me to discover that the baby wasn't mine. And there was no going back to the Guard. There we are. All caught up."

"I'm sorry. That's shitty."

"Yeah, it is. But you, Twinkle Toes, are going to get me back in the Guard, so you just point me in the direction of what or who I need to guard, and I'll take care of the rest."

"For what it's worth, she messed up. Anyone as determined as you to do something would have made a great father."

"Well, I guess I'll never know now."

She shrugged. "Come on, pretty boy, let's get to work."

JAX

Ariel wasn't kidding. She was starting fresh. While there was money for inventory like guns and surveillance equipment, we were light in inventory. We needed it shipped fast.

We spent the better part of the afternoon going through that. Then she had me speak to some mysterious friend of hers from New York, except the guy was a bit like me. Matthias something or other, he worked for a security firm in New York. They had some ridiculous tech on their hands. Earpieces that could barely be seen, bulletproof vests that were as thin as clothing, GPS trackers that could essentially be swallowed. Basically, they had access to the highest-grade military shit. The kind of shit that most of the world thought was science fiction.

The Royal Army and the Royal Guard were well kitted out. They had the latest in tech equipment, but even they didn't have stuff like this. We put in an order. Ariel had the funds, so that made things easy, but we still had to go through it all. When we were done, I had the night off. The following morning, we were supposed to head to one of our first assignments. Ariel had given me a couple of personnel files she wanted me to look over too. See everyone's strengths and weaknesses, where we could utilize everyone the best.

She had some guy coming in, Trace Lawson. His name was familiar, but I didn't know him. I still wasn't sure where I knew him from, but I'd look over his resume anyway. In the meantime, I might as well let the troops know I was back. When I texted Roone, he answered right away. "

Me: *Pub?*

Roone: *You back?*

Me: *Yep, just today.*

Roone: *Yeah, in an hour?*

Me: *Yep. Usual table?*

Roone: *Yeah, mate.*

Roone and I had developed a short hand working together. He'd been on the former prince's personal service for a long damn time. We'd all been on that rotation, those of us with exemplary test scores and excellent military service. We were all in rotation on the royal family themselves. Much like the American Secret Service, I suppose.

For the most part, Royal Guards were used for the royal family, no matter the level and distance to the throne, and members of the Regents Council. There were also Intelligence Guards, Palace Security, Diplomatic Guards, it went on and on. The most elite were Intelligence and Personal Guard for the royals. You pretty much wrote your own ticket at that point if you were so lucky as to be assigned those duties.

A couple of hours later, I borrowed one of the six SUV's in the garage. Ariel said they were for all of our use. I'd probably eventually get my own, but for now, the company SUV would suffice.

Parking was easy enough to find at the pub. I still slid into one of the spots hidden in the alley where I'd always parked. It was as if no one else on the island knew they were there.

That's because you had to have been drinking there for a long damn time to know about them. There'd been a fancy new parking lot built next to the pub four years ago. Only the locals new about these spots. Even then, most locals had graduated to more flashy pubs. But I liked this one. The Horse and Boar reminded me of pubs in London.

When I walked in through the back door, I spotted Roone immediately. He was at our old spot. The one where many of the Guards drank. And he'd already ordered two Guinness. Good man.

He grinned when he lifted his head and saw me. "Jax. Still a good-looking devil, I see."

"Ah, you flatter me. Careful now I'll get a swelled head. Now what will that pretty thing of yours say?"

Roone grinned. "She's beautiful, isn't she?"

I laughed. "Well, I only know from pictures. It's not like I've met her."

He winced. "Yeah, it was all kind of sudden. When we were in London I was undercover, so I couldn't exactly call. Then everything happened a bit fast. I didn't know you'd be back."

I waved my hand. "Nah, don't worry, just givin' you shit. I would love to meet the lost princess. From what I've seen in pictures, she's stunning."

The man was literally vibrating with light. He was so damn happy.

He shook his head. "Who'd have thought it?"

I laughed. "I know, right? You were the perpetual bachelor. I was the one careening toward love and family as quickly as possible."

He winced. "How are you doing?"

"Mate. I'm just gonna enjoy my pint and catch up with an old friend. We are not talking about her."

He shrugged. "All right, fair enough. But I mean, it is a valid question."

I rolled my eyes. "Okay, fine. Not gonna lie, it stung a bit.

Especially that she was a complete slag and made me walk away from my family. But I'm over it. Besides, you, mate, may have given me a way back."

Roone nodded slowly. "Hopefully it's a way back. Ariel and I will do our best. But you just focus on that job, let us worry about the rest. We'll have to get around the Council, and that's the tricky part."

"Look, I know. Your girl, Ariel, she already warned me it'd be a tough sell. I get it."

"How is that going? You getting on with her okay?"

I rolled my eyes. "Mate, she is a colossal pain in the ass."

Roone grinned. "I know, right? She's bossy. Thinks she should be in charge of everything."

I nodded enthusiastically. "Jesus Christ, she's persistent."

I thought back to the day that she was outside my flat banging to be let in at 6:00am.

He chuckled into his Guinness. "Oh, I know. She's a right pain in the ass. But she's good. Smarter than you. Smarter than everyone, basically, and she knows it. But she's a good partner. She's loyal. She'll do what it takes. Cover your ass no matter what. If you get into any trouble, she's the one you want on your team."

I studied him. "You almost sound like you love her."

He shrugged. "Yeah, I do. She's family."

"And the Princess isn't at all jealous?"

His brow burrowed. "Of Ariel? No. They're actually friends. Ariel was undercover with me."

"Oh, I didn't really know that, I guess."

"Yeah, it was a tough gig. Couldn't tell the princess a thing. We had to come out two pronged. She got to play good cop, I was bad cop."

"Yeah, obviously bad cop worked out."

"Yeah, but it almost didn't. Imagine calling my best mate having to tell him I got his sister killed."

I winced. "All turned out right?"

He shrugged and drained the rest of his beer. I was barely half done with mine. "Yeah it all turned out, but nothing's ever going to be the same. Everything is tense, and we're battling with the Regents Council. No one knows who to trust. When you have good people on your side, you keep them close."

I nodded slowly. "Ariel is one of the people you trust?"

He nodded. "Implicitly. She's had my life in her hands. She's had the princess's life in her hands. If she'd even hesitated, I'd be dead and so would the princess. I've been on the wrong end of a partner before. Didn't turn out well. Almost lost the prince."

I shook my head. "You know what, you have had some bad luck with assignments."

He chuckled. "Yeah, tell me about it."

"Seriously, maybe you need to retire."

He shrugged. "Yeah, I have given that some thought. But not yet. It's not my time. But you, you can't do better than Ariel. There are a couple of loopholes, we just need to figure out which play to make. But either way, she's good for her word."

I nodded slowly. "All right then. When am I going to meet this princess?"

It was good to see Roone. Good to remember why I loved being home so much. Being home was like sliding into warm sheets before going to bed, a sense of ease and familiarity. But I understood that this was an audition, so I wasn't going to fuck it up. I'd been making strides in my career when I quit to follow love. But I wasn't doing that shit again. I had a chance to get everything back. I wasn't going to give it up.

Chapter four

ARIEL

"Thank you for coming to see me."

I nodded. "This is a member of my team, Jax Reynolds."

"Mr. Reynolds."

Jax just nodded his head. Mr. Bipps indicated our seats, and we slid into them. The office was cozy but not cluttered. Dark furniture, well-made but worn. He'd clearly been in business a long time.

"What can we do for you?"

"Well, I've done some work for the crown."

I nodded slowly. Sebastian was keeping his word. I wasn't sure how I should feel about it, but I needed the help getting started, so I was going to take it. "Understood."

"You came highly recommended."

"Well, let's first see what we can do for you."

"I recently became the trustee for one of my clients. She passed away suddenly not too long ago."

"So sorry for your loss." I never knew what to say.

"Thank you. She's left behind a daughter and named a guardian for her."

"Is there a reason why you think either of them would need security?"

He shifted in his seat, then steepled his fingers as if he was trying to give me the no-frills response but was unsure how to deliver it. It was just a slight movement from left to right, as if he was wavering about how much to tell us.

"My client… Though her activities were not entirely illegal, I did worry about some of her clientele. She was a high-profile art dealer."

My brows raised. "Willa MacKenzie?"

He nodded. "You're familiar with her?"

"Well, just that she had the best parties on the island in her big fancy house up in Nob Hill. Parties that were impossible to get into. Any time there was a celebrity sighting, chances were he was off to one of Willa's parties."

"Yeah, that would be her. For the most part, her business was on the up and up. Obviously, I wouldn't work with anyone if they weren't."

I doubted that, but I urged him to continue. "Go on."

Next to me, I could see Jax grinding hard on his molars to keep from making some kind of retort.

"She had an accident. Single car, down the cliffs. She was quite wealthy, and she leaves substantial holdings behind. Her daughter is her sole heir."

I raised my brow. "And where is the father?"

"He's not named on the birth certificate and, according to Willa, not in the picture."

"Okay, so is the guardian a grandparent or something?"

He shook his head. "No. She's a friend of Willa's from childhood. My research into Miss Neela Wellbrook indicates that she is very much on the straight and narrow. Nothing questionable in her past or present. But I fear that she's ill-equipped to handle some of the responsibilities that might come along with being this baby's guardian."

Jax and I exchanged a look. "Mr. Bipps, it would be a lot faster for all of us if you spoke plainly."

He sighed then leaned forward, clasping his hands. "Fair enough. I'm certain some of Willa's clients might not be on the up-and-up. There was a lot of money changing hands. Some of her pieces are practically priceless. As a trustee, it's my job to ensure her daughter's future wealth. Someone might see her as a potential checkbook. I can't shake the feeling that someone is going to come for that kid. Kidnap and ransom, who knows? Her new guardian seems disinclined to heed my warnings, though."

Ah. I understood. "So, you want us to watch her without her knowing?"

He shrugged. "As it happens, she's in need of a nanny. She's looking for referrals. I was hoping you had someone on your staff who could double as both childcare and security."

I slowly glanced at Jax, who gave me a wide-eyed expression in return.

"Mr. Bipps, you're aware we're a small firm and we're just starting out. What you're speaking of will be long-term?"

"I'd like to say a minimum term of three months. Until everything's through probate and it's pretty clear that no one's coming after the kid. So yes, longer term."

"I don't have the staff for that."

Jax shifted in his chair. "How old's the kid?"

Mr. Bipps swung his gaze over to him. "Just a baby. Thirteen months."

Jax cursed under his breath before muttering, "I'll do it."

I blinked at him. "Do you have experience with kids?"

He shrugged. "I'm an uncle to seven. My sister practically lived with me when she had her oldest. She and her husband were going through a rough patch at the time. So yes, I'm well acquainted with diapers and making food. I'm also CPR certified."

I blinked at him. "Well, I didn't know that."

Mr. Bipps was as surprised as I was. "I was originally thinking Miss Scott, but I suppose there are male nannies." He eyed Jax more intensely now. "And I assume if Miss Scott has hired you, you are well acquainted with basic firearms and all that sort of thing, right?"

Jax raised a brow. "Yeah, I think I got that covered."

Mr. Bipps nodded enthusiastically as if the idea was taking hold and he was starting to like it. "Yes. This could work."

"Mr. Bipps, before you get too excited, I still only have one team member, and he will need a break. I still have a team to recruit."

"Yes, of course, I understand. But maybe if you could just go and meet with Ms. Wellbrook. I just have a bad feeling about the way Ms. MacKenzie died. So far it hasn't been ruled suspicious, and the roads had been a little wet from the night before, so it's entirely possible that she just went off the road. But I don't know. Something tells me there was more to it than that."

"Okay. I'll put Jax on it temporarily. Hopefully I can get the rest of my team together in the next week or two." I studied my partner in crime. "Can you do this?"

"Yeah. I got this. Kids are easy."

I sighed. "One of us is going to regret this. And luckily it won't be me." I was terrible with kids. They hated me. Babies especially. I had no idea what I was going to do when Penny and Sebastian finally had a kid. I could handle auntie duties, but prolonged tiny human contact, and I was toast.

"Mr. Bipps, I do suggest that perhaps you be searching for a more long-term solution. I would very much like the contract, but I'm just not sure we're your indefinite answer."

He nodded. "Understood. How about we call this a trial assignment. Three months and double your fee since it will require more than one team member to do a full assessment. If after three months you assess no threats toward Miss MacKenzie and Ms. Wellbrook, I will engage a more long-term solution."

I could work with that. Double our fee was hefty. That meant I could afford to pay Jax and the rest of the team without dipping so far into my reserves. At least while I got my other contracts going. "Fair enough. But may I suggest telling Ms. Wellbrook who we really are? Undercover work can get complicated."

I'd learned that the hard way. When Penny had gone undercover to guard the king, then prince, lines had gotten blurry really quick. The same for when Roone had been sent to guard the lost princess. It just always got messy. I'd been behind keeping Sebastian in the dark the first time. But after seeing how that almost cost him and Penny each other, I was on team bare-it-all now.

He shook his head. "She's putting her foot down and insisting she doesn't need security. But my guess is she doesn't understand exactly the kind of lifestyle Ms. MacKenzie led. I'd rather be safe than sorry."

"Okay. Give us the address and we'll go meet with her." I turned to Jax. "Look like you're her new manny."

He scowled at me. "You are not calling me that."

I grinned in response. "Oh no, on the contrary. That's your new nickname."

I just hoped that I was right about this job. I didn't usually like to put untried people in undercover roles, but if the client was insisting, we had to do what he asked. Besides, Jax Reynolds had a goal. He wasn't going to mess that up by shagging the client.

Chapter
five

NEELA

could do this. She was just a baby. Babies were sweet... and cute... and had the propensity to try and kill themselves on a daily basis.

After leaving Mr. Bipps's office, I'd made a quick call to work and left a message for Bex and Adam to call me. Then I'd headed straight for the new house.

I'd chosen to have Child Protective Services meet me at the house in Nob Hill. At least it would be familiar to Mayzie. But maybe that was a mistake.

It was too weird being there without Willa.

The woman from Child Protective Services was brisk and no-nonsense. She was all battle axe. Short, stout, built like a brick shit house. Stern face. Hawk-like nose. A narrowed gaze that told me she saw everything. But the way Mayzie clung to her, you would think that she was Mayzie's mother.

I gave her a tremulous smile. "Hi. I guess you're here for me."

My attempt at humor was not met with a smile. Instead, she indicated her assistant behind her. He was thin with longish hair and brown skin. "This is Thomas. He has your paperwork, Ms. Wellbrook. There will be a schedule for child visits. We will inspect the home and the support system you've built for Mayzie.

I nodded as she spoke. She was saying words like *check-ups*, and *appointments*, and all these important sounding things. But I couldn't focus. My gaze was glued to the baby in her arms. The baby who was half asleep but looked like she did not intend to go anywhere.

There was also *stuff* that came with the baby. There was a stroller and a duffel bag slung over old Battle Axe's shoulder. Thomas held a box of snacks, some well-used books, and a stuffed toy or two.

"Are those her things?"

Battle Axe gave me a short nod. "Yes. When we were notified of Ms. MacKenzie's death, we packed a few things from the house. Since you're back in the home, Mayzie should feel more comfortable."

Just that morning, I'd signed documents to remove Richard from my accounts. And then I'd signed the guardianship documents. Severing one relationship and starting a whole new one.

"Of course. Right."

Old Battle Axe eyed me up and down.

"I'm going to hand her to you now. This is a good time to ask any questions."

I stared at her and then stared at Mayzie, half praying that she wouldn't give me the baby.

I hadn't been this terrified in years. Not since Tom Wells had asked me to the senior prom. In the end, it turned out he'd really wanted to go with Willa instead, so I'd backed down and she'd gone with him.

"Here she is."

Battle Axe was holding out Mayzie, who was struggling in her arms and looked like she was trying to hold on to her baby-koala style.

Poor thing. I reached my arms out and took the squirming baby.

"Hey, sweetheart. I'm your Auntie Neela. I'm going to be hanging out and taking care of you from now on. You think that might work for a little while?"

Mayzie blinked up at me with big green eyes and impossibly long lashes. Her little nose scrunched up and she blinked several times as if assessing me. And then her forehead furrowed and she sniffed. And then out came the wail.

A wail of severe protest as if I had taken away her binky. What in the world had I agreed to?

Battle Axe said nothing. Just handed over the duffel bag and the paperwork.

"We'll be back to check on you in a couple of days. Best you two get acquainted."

I tried to rock Mayzie in my arms and soothe her, but Mayzie was not having it. The screeching only grew louder.

"Jesus, I just got you. I don't know what you need. When did you last eat?"

She's not going to talk to you, dumbass. She's a baby.

I lifted her, wrinkling my nose as I sniffed her bottom. She was dry, and there were no surprises in there. So maybe she was hungry?

I opened the duffel bag and pulled out a bottle that looked

like formula. I tested it on my wrist as I'd seen done on television. Then I stuffed the bottle into Mayzie's little wailing mouth.

Two little teeth peeped out at me from the bottom of her gums, and I was struck by how adorable they were.

At first, Mayzie rejected the bottle and shook her little head back and forth. "Look, I know. I clearly don't know what I'm doing. But right now, it's you and me, so we need to figure this shit out. If you're not hungry, tell me. Do you just need to be held? Just tell me. Do you like the rocking?"

Jesus, I'd already Auntie failed and sworn in front of the baby. I bounced up and down with her a little bit. She did quiet down a little and then snuffled. It was as if she had to stop crying to realize that there was milk in her mouth. Then she immediately started suckling. Her little chubby, dimpled hands reached up to smack the bottle, as if willing it to go faster.

I sighed, relief rushing through my veins as she quieted.

"Thank God."

I held her close and smoothed her hair off her forehead. "I'm really happy to meet you. Your mama was one of my oldest friends. More like family, actually. And I miss her already."

Mayzie blinked back at me as she ate. She looked just like Willa, and I fought the pang of grief. I had to keep my shit together. I could do this. I would not fail this little girl. Not the way I'd been failed. I was going to give her what she needed.

And what about what you need?

What I needed didn't matter. The rest of my life might be in shambles, but holding Mayzie in my arms felt like the best decision I'd made in years.

"Well, Mayzie, it looks like we're not in Kansas anymore. But I think you and I… we've got this."

NEELA

I most decidedly did not have *shit*.

After two days of the demon baby who refused to sleep, I was ready to throw in the towel. Under normal circumstances, I wasn't a quitter. Not by any means. I was the woman who never said die. But that baby, she was killing my will to live.

Oh, she was the sweetest, most beautiful girl I'd ever laid eyes on, but she was a handful. For starters, she refused to sleep if she wasn't in my bed.

And then there was the little matter of her refusing to eat anything. The only thing she voluntarily ate was her milk. She loved that. And apparently, avocado. Everything else was met with disdain. And considering there were shelves and shelves of all kinds of baby food in the pantry, I knew it was food she was used to.

Her mother just died. Cut the baby some slack.

Bullshit. What about my slack?

God, I was so tired. I needed to focus on getting some paying clients. Or getting the clients I had to give me more work. Hell, at this point, I'd have been happy with a shower. I was exhausted, and it was showing.

Mayzie cried constantly. She was a baby, so at least that part I was expecting. But I didn't know how to fix it.

It was the hardest two days of my life. My usual, no-nonsense attitude of making a plan, sticking to the plan, executing the plan, and delivering it on time and within budget did not apply to babies.

I didn't know what day it was, I didn't know what time it was, and I was quite certain I was missing a meeting.

I rushed at the door to my office, Mayzie in tow, certain I was late for an appointment. I had looked this morning as I was leaving, checking my schedule, and saw that at nine a.m. I had a meeting I couldn't remember setting up.

Which was horrible. I possibly had a new client, which would be good for business, and I was already making a crappy first impression.

Bex and Adam had stepped up, but I couldn't do another day of this. I needed that damn nanny. I handed Mayzie off to Bex. "Okay, she's had milk this morning. Please see if you can get her to eat some of those peas or whatever. And then if you could just—"

Bex interrupted. "I've got it under control already. Adam and I moved—"

And I interrupted her as I was peeling off my coat and shaking off the morning's drizzle. "I don't even know who's in my office right now. Do I have a file to prepare?"

She shook her head. "No, I moved your meeting that was supposed to be 9:30 to make room for this one. These are the people Mr. Bipps sent over."

Thank fuck. The nanny agency.

Bex and Adam exchanged looks. I knew what I looked like. My blouse didn't quite go with this blazer, but it had been the only spare one I had in the car because, of course, Mayzie had spat up as I was getting her out of the car.

So I'd had to put her back in her car seat and change quickly in the garage before I came up. "Okay, she must be teething or something because she's been gnawing on her—"

"Go. You have a meeting." Bex looked at Mayzie, who, traitorous little baby that she was, practically snuggled into Bex's arms and started cooing. *Demon hellspawn.*

Why was it so easy for Bex?

I didn't have time for that thought. I had a potential savior in my office. I needed to convey a cool and professional vibe, not one as a desperate mother of hellspawn.

I shoved open my office door and froze.

There was a man inside. A *large* man. And from his profile, I could tell that he was a *holy shit never seen anyone so hot* kind of attractive man. I quickly whipped around to glare at Bex for not warning me, and she shrugged, mouthing at me, "Go."

I turned back around. How was this guy the nanny?

"Um, excuse me. Do you know if this is a mistake?"

His smile was brief as he turned his body. The small movement blocked out the streaks of sunlight into my office. He was tall for sure. Well over six feet was my estimate. But he was mostly lean. Except for his shoulders.

I swallowed around the sawdust in my mouth. Holy freaking hell. Nannies did not look like this man. Nannies were pleasantly curved with wide smiles and soft voices and could endure endless hours of Elmo songs.

This man looked like he might *shoot* Elmo.

He was talking. There were words, and they were coming out of his mouth, and his voice was... feminine? What? No. His lips weren't moving. So then, who the hell was doing the talking?

He stepped aside, and all of a sudden, I could breathe again. Once he was out of my line of sight, all the air came whooshing back into my lungs.

There was a woman behind him. She'd just been hidden by his massive shoulders.

She stepped forward with a smile. "Ms. Wellbrook, it's nice to meet you."

I blinked rapidly. "Oh, yes, nice to meet you too." Had she said their names? My mind was drawing a complete blank. I'd been too busy ogling the giant gorgeous man, and I'd completely missed it.

"I'm sorry, what was your name again?"

Her smile was warm, but she didn't look any more like a nanny than the badass with the model's face. "I'm Ariel Scott. My associate's name is Jax Reynolds. Mr. Bipps sent us."

I shook her hand. Firm. Warm. No nonsense. I got the impression she was a straight shooter and direct. While those were qualities I admired in a business relationship, they were not exactly ones ideal for a baby.

I braced myself to shake Jax's hand. It didn't do any good. A jolt of electricity zinged up my arm. When he spoke, his voice rumbled, like a big cat purring. I had to focus to hear the words. "It's a pleasure, ma'am."

Christ on a cracker, he was British. At least his accent was. The islands boasted many an ex-pat.

With the low timbre and the accent, he could very well have said 'I'd like to lick you now, ma'am,' and I wouldn't have known the difference.

His hand nearly enveloped mine, holding on for a second too long. Eyes the color of the Caribbean waters I'd loved my whole life, held my gaze.

Lord, that gaze. He was the kind of guy that kept his eyes open during sex. He certainly would never miss a single detail.

I needed to talk. Words in this moment would be great. Just because they didn't look like nannies didn't mean they didn't have a nanny company and weren't trying to figure out my needs.

Libido: *I'm sure he can figure out your needs.*

Thank Christ he couldn't hear what I was thinking. Or worse, see the scenes my imagination was conjuring up. It had been a long, long time since I'd had sex, and Jax Reynolds was ticking off every damn fantasy box.

"Right, okay then. Have a seat."

They both took theirs, and just as I was about to take mine, I could hear Mayzie's displeased wail coming from the other room.

Damn.

Was she hurt? Did she need more formula? Should I go out and mix it for her? Had she lost Mr. Ta? Mr. Ta was a sensory toy that looked like a butterfly. Parts of him crinkled. Other parts of him had zippers and buttons. Mostly, Mayzie chewed his face. She always called him *Ta*, so I assumed his name was Mr. Ta.

I hesitated again but reminded myself Bex could handle her for thirty minutes. It would be fine. How did moms do this all the time? Every little wail. Every little cry. It was nerve fraying.

I forced myself into my seat. Bex knew what to do. Mayzie would be fine.

Ariel sat forward. "Mr. Bipps spoke with me, of course. I think Royal Elite could be what you need, but it would be helpful to hear from you exactly what you're looking for."

Royal Elite? Something told me this agency might be out of my price range.

Except you have money specifically for this.

I forced my shoulders to relax again. "Okay. Well I think that—"

More wailing from the outer office. Ariel and Jax turned their gazes toward the door. "If you need to get her, we understand."

I resisted the urge to run out there to solve whatever ailment Mayzie had. "No. Bex will handle it. So, I was saying, obviously, you can see that I need—"

Full-scale tantrum crying had erupted.

I stood, but Jax beat me to it. In less than three strides he was at the door and had it open. I heard the low murmur of his voice. "There, there. That's a love." The crying stopped immediately.

Moments later, Jax was back with Mayzie and her diaper bag in tow. Without a word to either of us, he found a flat surface on top of my low book shelves, took out the changing pad, and changed her diaper quickly. No muss, no fuss.

What sorcery was this?

Ariel and I just stared. Jax carried her back to us and sat down with her on his lap, then nodded at me. "Carry on. Poor love was just wet. No one likes a wet arse."

I blinked at him then at the baby. "You're hired." I didn't give two shits that he didn't look how I expected a nanny to look. He'd just made Mayzie a happy camper. I'd check all their references, call Mr. Bipps and confirm, but it looked like I had just hired my new manny.

Chapter six

JAX

Get your shit together.

Holy hell. What the fuck had just happened in there?

It had all been so simple. Walk in there, ask the client what she needed from us, get a schedule.

All I had to do was follow the script. But then she walked in, and every cell in my body had screamed GTFO. *Danger, asshole, danger.*

I'd been ready to comply with the command, but then her dark-as-sin eyes had met mine, and holy fuck me. It was as if someone had sucked the air out of the room.

Want.

It was a single thought. Nothing extra or flowery added. It was clear. Direct. Uncomplicated. And way the fuck off limits. I wanted her so bad it sucker-punched me.

Lucky for me, she'd turned her attention to Ariel. I'd been given some reprieve to think, but all the blood had already rushed to my cock, so the last brain cell I had working had a bitch of a time firing.

After I'd gotten the baby, Ariel had gone over schedule and coverage with her. I'd be moving into her house, which was trouble. But I wasn't going to call attention to it. When we had additional team members, we'd rotate out as necessary.

I still wasn't sure how the hell Neela Wellbrook was going to believe we were a bunch of nannies, since basically anyone Ariel hired would telegraph as badass. But that was Ariel's problem not mine. I still didn't know why we couldn't just be upfront with her. In my experience, it would have made it easier on the client.

I wasn't sure what the fuck I'd been expecting from coming home and taking this job, but whatever it was, Neela Wellbrook, wasn't it. Wasn't I already in this shit because of a woman? Well, two women if I was counting Ariel, who at the moment was silent as a tomb.

Her silence suited me fine. She'd noticed. How could she not notice? I'd had the subtlety of a rude-boy at a grime concert.

Back to my earlier point of needing to get my shit together. Just because Neela had eyes that could see clear to my soul, and smooth, tanned skin that looked softer than satin, and a backbone strong enough to challenge someone like me...

You can't have her.

I knew the rules. I knew the plan. I had a goal. I was going to get my life back. I could keep my shit in check. I was there for the baby. Poor little mite had just been wet. And Neela's employees clearly had no idea what to do with a baby.

"You and I are on the same page, right?"

Fuck. Had she been talking? "Same page?"

Ariel hooked a left on King's Road. "Yeah. Where's your head at? I know she said we'd officially start on Monday, but as of right now, you're on the clock. I want you to keep an eye on her until then. The lawyer is concerned. So, I'm concerned until I have reason not to be."

I'd keep an eye on her all right. "Full coverage?"

She shook her head. "No, just on the road. To and from appointments and things for now. I have a feeling about this one."

I narrowed my gaze at her. "A feeling?"

She nodded. "Yeah. I've learned to listen to my gut by this point. Everything I've seen in the last few years taught me to be sure. I've already downloaded her schedule to the tablet, so you'll be able to cover her."

I knew from my research that Ariel was a hell of a hacker. "Should I ask how you got that information?"

"Probably best if you don't."

"Fine. Will do. When will you be back?"

"Couple of days. In the meantime, I have a list of clients whose needs I want you to assess. It's mainly phone calls. Can you manage that?"

"Got you, Red. This is your show."

Her nod was brusque as she made a turn for the airport exit. "Yeah about this being my show. I need you to keep your dick in your pants around Neela Wellbrook. I've seen too many good men distracted and making rash decisions because they don't have enough blood left in their brains to think."

So she *had* caught that. "She won't be a problem."

"It's not her I'm worried about."

I clicked my jaw shut. "Yeah, I hear you."

"Uh-huh. I'd believe you more if you didn't sound like the big bad wolf when you said it."

ARIEL

I didn't exactly trust Jax to heed my warnings, but I didn't really have any choice. I needed to go on my next recruiting mission, and he was the man I had on the ground.

Thanks to the crown, I was headed right back for the private jet. As the golf cart drove me out on the tarmac, I looked back at the SUV I'd left back in the parking lot. Jax was folding his big body into the driver's seat, and I was wondering if I'd made a mistake. The way he looked at Neela spelled trouble. A part of me thought he might eat her right there, never mind that I was in the room. Because hey, who doesn't love an audience?

I shook my head and turned my attention back to my phone. *Trace.*

Trace Lawson. He'd been in the military with Sebastian and Roone, but he hadn't been Royal Guard. Looking through his file, it looked like had family. A little sister. He'd need to have a more regular schedule and be available for her.

So he was a good option. His sister was fifteen now, a sophomore in high school. He'd have to start thinking about university. And I was certainly paying well.

The golf cart stopped at the plane. The stairs were already down, and the pilot waved at me as I said, "I swear to God we've got to stop meeting like this."

His smile was warm. "It's nice to see you again, Miss Scott. We're all fueled and ready to go when you are."

I nodded. "Thank you. Hopefully it'll just be the one stop."

"As His Majesty said, I am at your disposal whenever you need me."

It did pay to have friends in high places. But the last thing on earth I wanted to do was take advantage. The sooner I got this done and had my team in place the better.

I didn't really care where I sat on the plane. I picked the first seat I saw, plunked my bag into the seat next to it, flopped right in, and then jammed on my seatbelt.

I hated take offs. To me, it was the worst part of flying. I always felt like the plane might break. To distract myself, I started scrolling through my emails.

When my Google alert dinged, my stomach cramped automatically. I knew what that meant. I didn't want to look. At the same time, it was an impulse. I couldn't stop myself. I knew that only pain would come with looking. I knew how I would feel for the next several days after looking. It still didn't stop me, though.

I used to play this game with myself whenever they would come in. Give myself a little reward if I went 30 seconds without looking, a minute, five. One time I even went a whole two hours. Granted, I'd been in the middle of a debrief at the time. But still, I got huge ass reward then. That one involved lots of liquor.

Do not look. As a matter of fact, turn off the alerts.

But I knew I was kidding myself. I was going to look. And no way in hell was I turning off those alerts. They were my only connection to former me. The part of me that still had a heart. They were the only connection to my past. I couldn't let them go. No matter how much I tried.

You are an idiot. He's not coming back. None of that is ever happening. You need to move on.

Penny, Bryna, Jinx and Jessa were all on me that I needed to try online dating. Hell, I even had my own app for that. Problem was I knew how many crazies were out there. A little light hacking and I could actually see what they were hiding.

Having that much information at my fingertips was

exhausting, it was also terrifying. I felt like online dating would work better if you could believe the lies someone told you upfront. Like I work here. I have this exciting job. I'm a good person. I won't leave you high and dry.

I love you.

All kinds of lies. And I was the moron who was prone to believing them.

One guy. One time. Cut yourself some slack.

There would be no slack cutting. And as the plane started to taxi onto the runway, sure enough, I checked my Google alert.

Prince Tristan of the Winston Isles was out on the town with his fiancée, Ella Tisdale, at the opera during a benefit for the Clean Water Project. The beautiful couple were wearing Korgin James and Draco, looking very much in love.

Gut punch.

It had been nearly a decade, but it still hurt because I was an idiot. But it was the article I saw next that had my eyes focusing in on it. *A disturbance at the opera where Prince Tristan of the Winston Isles was in attendance. News story developing.*

A disturbance?

I spent the next five minutes down a rabbit hole. I couldn't escape from reports of gunfire at the Vienna State Opera in Austria following a fundraiser. Prince Tristan's soccer team had been honored for their charity work.

It didn't say who'd been shot or if anyone had been hurt at all. Fear gripped me like a cold fist around my stomach. Had he been hurt? After his brother's betrayal of the crown, the whole family had been in a kind of exile outside of public life for the most part, and they had decreased security because of those circumstances. They were each assigned one guard. That was all the Council would allow.

Why can't you let this guy go?

Because there was a part of me that was still holding onto him.

You can't do it. Let it go. Shut it down.

That time, I listened. I closed the app and leaned back. It was a gossip site. Who knew if it was even true? More than likely, someone's car had backfired, and here I was eating it up.

I went to Google and pulled up my alerts. My finger hovered over the *off/on* switch. This time I was going to turn it off. This time I could manage it. But before I could force my finger to press *off*, I chickened out. *Again.*

Finally, I closed down the app, chucked my phone into my bag, and deliberately clipped it shut. No more. Not today. I couldn't take it.

Chapter seven

NEELA

'd made a mistake.

What in the world had possessed me to tell Royal Elite I didn't need them until Monday?

You wanted to do your research on them.

All I'd found was a website with pictures of happy looking babies and parents on it with testimonials. Mr. Bipps had provided me references, and they'd checked out.

"So let me get this straight. You hired that fine specimen of man as your manny, and then you told him not to start until *Monday?*"

I groaned. "I know. I know. I was having reservations and thought maybe a couple of days to check everything would do me some good."

"What reservations? That man was amazing with Mayzie. And amazing to look at. You deserve some eye candy," Bex said with a wicked gleam in her eye.

"I don't know. It all happened in a blur. He was too much, too intense. So I said 'you're hired,' but then I freaked out and said 'Start Monday,' completely forgetting that I'd be on my own for four more days. And I don't know. Don't you get the impression he's bossy? Like authoritative. I don't think I'd like bossy." I had zero to go on, except that intense way he watched me. There was something about him that said he was used to being in charge.

I adjusted Mayzie on my hip as I checked the diaper bag. I needed some fresh air. When I was little and had a bad day or was sad, my father used to take me down to Prince's Beach, and we'd walk the promenade, eat enough gelato to put a six-year-old into a sugar coma, and talk. We'd stay out until I'd at least giggled a dozen times. It was also where he'd walk me through puzzles. They were a surefire way to calm my brain. It was the one time I hadn't noticed the constant presence of armed guards.

Whenever my life was in disarray, I still went for that little walk. Kind of like now.

Bex saw me struggling and rolled her eyes. She grabbed the bag and shoved the essentials inside.

"So what if the man is bossy. Did you see how hot he was? He could boss me around anytime with that voice. Holy mercy. I'm good at taking orders. Also, he got Mayzie to stop crying."

Mayzie gurgled and slapped my boob. "Sorry kid, nothing is coming out of there. But if you need a bottle, I've got you covered."

"Don't you dare deflect with the baby. There was a hot man in here, way hotter than Richard."

"It's not like he was here for a date, Bex. He's my new manny, so he's way the hell off-limits. He's here for Mayzie. Thanks to Willa, she is my priority now. Not my lady parts."

Bex rolled her lips then and said nothing. She and Willa had not gotten along. Bex had always thought that Willa took me for granted and insisted on always shining, never letting me step front and center.

I didn't necessarily agree with that, but Bex was entitled to her own opinion, and she was protective of me. Willa had been protective of me too, in her own way. But I couldn't help but agree that *sometimes*, Willa had stepped on me so that she would be seen instead.

"Sounds like Willa, leaving you to clean up her messes again."

"I know you didn't like her—"

"That's an understatement."

I put Mayzie in her stroller and strapped her in. "But she's Mayzie's mom, or rather, she was. And like her or not, we have to do what's best for Mayzie. Even if she won't sleep and refuses to eat anything I give her. Willa is gone, so I need to give Mayzie the best. And right now, apparently, it's the hot manny."

Bex's lip twitched. "So, you noticed he was hot?"

"My eyes are in perfect working order. But I don't even know what to do with a man that hot."

Bex guffawed. "Oh, I know what to do with him. It's going to involve honey, some ice cubes, and handcuffs."

I nearly choked on the coffee I sipped. "Oh my God, I don't even want to know."

She grinned at me. "Are you sure you don't want to know? Because maybe you could use some pointers. You know, get the lead out."

"I do not need to *get the lead out.*"

She rolled her eyes. "Yes, you do. Especially when you were dating *Dick.*"

"*Richard.*" I put my hands over Mayzie impressionable little ears. "Little ears."

"She can't talk yet."

"But this is when she's learning. Formative years." It occurred to me that Bex and I were going to have to clean up our language.

"That's his name, *Dick*. He told me to call him Dick. Who says that? Also, he actually *is* a dick. That's just the truth. I mean, I've never met a man more threatened by a powerful woman."

I laughed. "I'm hardly powerful. I have no idea how we're going to pay rent on this place."

She winced. "About that. The property manager called. It looks like *Dick* never paid last month's rent."

Damn it. "I'll figure it out."

"I know that's your motto and everything, but you have to let Adam and me help."

"You guys *are* helping. Something has to give. I didn't even get a chance to think through everything. It all happened so quickly. Then Mayzie landed in my lap. I promise I'll find a solution."

Bex checked her watch. "Oops, I've got to go. Adam has been on the phones. I know he had some hot dinner date with his girlfriend. Why don't you take the rest of the afternoon off? You don't have any more meetings, and you've been burning the midnight oil if the emails are any indication."

"Well, I have to put that pitching proposal together for Miami Code Machine. I'll maybe do that from ho—" I stopped myself. Willa's house wasn't home.

It is for Mayzie.

"I'll do it from Willa's."

Bex tossed her empty latte cup into the trash can we passed. "Are we just not going to talk about the fact that you actually have a lot of money now? And you can afford to be picky about clients?"

"It's not *my* money Bex. It's Mayzie's. I really don't want it."

She sighed. "Fine, be that way. But you get a stipend to look after Mayzie, and looking after her means looking after yourself too. That might be just what you need to get on your feet."

As I pushed the stroller, I considered what Bex said. I hadn't even looked over the trust documents yet. My life had been diapers and baby food and adjustments for the last three days.

In that three days, I'd given up my flat because even if I didn't want the Nob Hill house, it made no sense trying to drag poor Mayzie into a one bedroom flat.

But I needed to make some fast decisions. The current office space was too big for the three of us. It was also more than I could afford.

Adam and I had called each of our remaining clients to pitch them on more work. A few had come through, but not enough to keep us going *and* pay rent.

One idea that had been rattling around in my head was moving the company to the guest house at Willa's. It had enough room, and it was just the three of us. Adam and I could take client work and there would be no rent, which meant I could pay my team. Plus, there was the added benefit of being near Mayzie.

I pushed along the pathway headed west toward Prince's Beach that would cut through the oldest, most touristy part of Old Town. Most of the capital city was extremely modern, the king wanting the islands to be a true comfort destination. But this part of the city was my favorite. It was so full of color and life.

As I walked, I talked to Mayzie. These moments when everything was peaceful and I had sort of figured her out for the day were the perfect moments. They were the brief spans of time when I believed I could do this. That I could keep her happy and take care of her. Unfortunately, they were also the times when I thought of Willa and what she would want me to do with her daughter.

She's your daughter now.

A fact I didn't think I'd ever get used to.

Mayzie cooed as I pointed out some of the birds as we passed through Old Town. Constant baby talk was exhausting. I was running out of things to say. I was so glad I had Bex and Adam to talk to, otherwise constant baby babble would make me insane.

The hairs at the back of my neck stood up, and I paused, glancing around. I had that feeling of someone watching me. I hated to admit it to Bex, but I'd had that feeling for a couple of days now, which was silly as we had already discussed the fact that nobody cared about me.

I don't know what made me do it, but I took a left, passing through a row of tucked away shops on a cobbled street that was far too narrow for cars, and I picked up my pace.

But the faster I walked, the more that alarm trailed along the nape of my neck down in my arms and my legs. Before I knew it, my heart hammered, and I was moving quickly. So quickly I was practically running with the stroller.

Why are you running?

Because some part of my lizard brain had registered danger, and I knew that I had to protect the baby. I didn't know how I knew. I just *knew*.

So I moved my ass faster than it had probably moved in months. I'd let my gym membership lapse because all my time had gone into the company.

I wished I hadn't let that happen, because all those moms

with their jogging strollers, *those* women looked in shape. *I* was not.

I ducked into a shop and pulled the stroller in with me. The owner frowned at me and rolled her eyes. The stroller was clearly too wide to fit through the aisles of the tiny boutique, but I needed a place to rest and pull out my phone.

I was ready to call the police just in case, but mostly I was hiding out, blending in. Waiting for the big bad boogeyman to announce himself.

But nobody passed, except for people who looked like other shoppers.

Mayzie clapped her hands and pulled at a bright pink top with fur where the boobs would be. Mayzie felt it up and cooed and giggled. *Fantastic.* And of course, there was drool all over her mouth.

I smiled at the owner and pointed at the blouse. "How much? She just seems to love it."

"It's a hundred and fifteen dollars."

My brows dropped. "What?"

It had sheer sleeves, basic cotton for a bodice, and fur on the boobs. How did it have enough fabric to equal a hundred and fifteen dollars? I took it off the hanger, handed it to Mayzie, and pulled out my credit card.

Mayzie had already drooled all over it, so there wasn't any way I could say I wasn't going to buy it.

Once I'd paid for my impromptu purchase, Mayzie laughed and rubbed at the fur happily.

"I have an awful suspicion you have a terrible sense of fashion."

She didn't answer.

I stepped back out of the boutique and headed back the way we'd come.

When I passed the next alley, someone reached out and grabbed my arm. I opened my mouth to scream, not sure if I should pull Mayzie with me or push her away so that somebody would see her and call the police. But before I could get a sound out, a hand clamped over my mouth. *Hard.*

I bit the hand and heard the muttered curse behind me. Then the hand was back, but I was already running and held on to the stroller. I had to get more momentum.

The man behind me grabbed again. "Just tell us where it is, and we'll let you go."

Where what was? I tried to remember the self-defense classes my father had insisted I take when I was young. Stomp the instep. I tried that, but I couldn't get leverage. I had the stroller and the diaper bag.

Shit. Instep. Instep. What was instep again?

Top of the foot. Right.

My brain was so unhelpful in these circumstances.

"Tell us where it is."

I opened my mouth and tried to bite him again. That earned me a whack on the back of the head. It wasn't too hard, but still, it hurt enough to startle me. "I don't know what you're talking about."

He leaned forward. "Bite me again, and I swear to God I'm going to take that baby."

I opened my mouth to scream. "Hheeeel—"

The hand clamped back over my mouth again.

I let go of the stroller this time and fought like hell. I slammed my head back. I tried to use my arms to whack him in the nuts, but all I got was upper thigh.

The next thing I knew, the hand over my mouth went slack and then the body behind me was moving back, releasing me.

I grabbed on to Mayzie's stroller and tried to start pushing, but the stupid thing had locked on me. I used my foot to try to pry the lock up. Mayzie, thankfully, had no idea anything was wrong, so she just gurgled.

"Move. Come on, move."

And then there was another voice behind me, low and menacing… and… familiar. I'd been playing it in my head for the last day. "Relax. You're okay. He's not going to hurt you."

I whipped around and used my body to block the stroller, hands up, as if *I* could do anything.

Jax Reynolds had *removed* whoever had grabbed me. He'd done something to him, because that guy lay in a heap by the bins, presumably passed out. Shit was he dead? I didn't think he'd kill anyone in broad daylight. Or would he?

"I will scream."

He held his hands up. "Eyes on me. You're okay. Pull out your phone. Call the police."

I stared at him. "The police? You want me to call the police?"

He nodded slowly. "You're in shock. As you should be. But this gentleman here just tried to grab you off the street in broad daylight. So generally, people call the police."

I frowned. "The police, right." My hands shook. I could barely function. I couldn't put two words together.

He reached out a hand and beckoned with his fingers. "Give it here."

I didn't have any choice. There was no way I could dial.

He dialed the police, and then he murmured our location and that he was a concerned bystander. He didn't give his name before he hung up.

"The police are on their way. Okay?"

I stared at him.

"I need you to nod or something to let me know you understand."

Finally, I was able to move my head up and down.

"Okay. Come on over here. Have a seat."

I obeyed on autopilot. He'd saved me. He had saved me and Mayzie from whoever the hell that was.

I swayed on my feet. He reached for me, and I was going to let him catch me. I really was. But then the stupid stroller started to roll, and when I reached for it, I lost my footing and fell forward, my hands grabbing out for leverage. I caught his belt as his arm reached out to break my fall.

Fat load of good it did me, my face found a good landing place.

In his crotch.

It seemed Jax Reynolds was big... *everywhere*.

He looked down at me warily with a wide smirk. "Usually women buy me dinner before asking to see the goods, but in your case, I'll make an exception."

My face flamed.

I tried to talk, but Lord! My eyes were completely, utterly focused on his massive—

He snapped his fingers in front of my eyes. "Hey, Neela—Ms. Wellbrook. My eyes, they're up here. Give me your hand."

Oh my God. If it was possible to die of mortification, I needed that shit to happen right now.

Come on, gods. Any second now.

Apparently, the gods were not listening because no one smote me, or struck me with lightning, or anything of the sort. I had no choice but to take his hand and let him help me up.

I whipped around and checked for Mayzie. She started to make the *uhuh-uhuh* sound. I knew that sound by now. Tears were incoming.

With practiced ease, he reached in, unsnapped Mayzie, and held her close, then maneuvered me to the sidewalk and wrapped an arm around me too, cocooning me.

That small motion chased away the chill and fear.

JAX

She might be a giant pain in the ass, but my new boss had one hell of an instinct.

"Good job on Neela Wellbrook. Any ID on the twat-buster who tried to jump her?"

Ariel was seated across from me at the glass conference table at Royal Elite. The police had people up at Neela's new place for the night, but I'd feel a hell of a lot better once we were done and I could get up there.

My brain oh-so-helpfully kept replaying what had happened, as if I needed that visual. I didn't want to think about what would have happened if I hadn't been there. I'd heard that guy say he wanted something from her or he was going to take the baby. She hadn't seemed to know what he wanted.

"Thanks. It was the right call to stay on her. The guy is a ghost. Not in any database the police have. And he's not talking."

She sighed. "I might have my own look at his fingerprints. My last gig taught me to me suspicious of everyone."

While she spoke, Ariel's new recruit sized me up.

He was a big guy who moved like he knew what the fuck he was doing, though he had an air to him that seemed easygoing. But there was something in his eyes that said he didn't fuck with assholes.

Blond, blue-eyed, pretty-boy surfer type. Had he been in the Guard to? I didn't remember him. I wondered what leverage she'd used to get him here. Given his accent, it was unlikely he had been Guard.

Ariel finished typing something into her laptop then glanced up, catching us eyeing each other.

"Jax, Trace Lawson. Trace, Jax Reynolds."

We both nodded at each other as we tried to determine pecking order on the team.

I leaned forward. "Okay, if we're going back tonight, I need to know the plan."

Ariel pulled the open the schematics for Neela Wellbrook's home on the large screen in the office. "How many men do you think you'll need?"

"I'm not sure yet. For now, I'll keep the current gate staff. It's just the two rotational guards. I looked up the company that provides the guards, and they seem above board. No problems. If you can dig into Neela Wellbrook's background to see if there is anyone that would want to hurt her, that would be helpful."

"I'm already on it. So far, she's squeaky clean. There was an ex. A *recent* ex, from what I can tell, but he's mostly just a douche bag. His name, if you can believe it, is Richard Dickson."

I lifted my brows. "Dick Dickson?"

Ariel snorted a laugh. "I know, right? That's just the icing on the cake."

Trace shook his head and chuckled. "That's the douchiest name I've ever heard."

" I need to meet this wanker."

Ariel continued. "From the looks of it, he's just an average guy. He and Neela used to work together, and it ended badly. Some kind of power struggle over the company."

Trace took the file on Dick Dickson. "So basically, prime suspect number one?"

Ariel shook her head. "Normally, yes. But in this case, it doesn't seem like it. Neela is a cryptanalyst. Her company is a consultancy firm that helps companies and government organizations safeguard and protect themselves with high level encryptions."

I frowned. "So she's a hacker like you?"

Ariel grinned. "Sweetheart, I'm so much more than a hacker. I look real nice with a gun too."

Trace chuckled.

"But Neela's more than a hacker."

I shook my head. "Give me the kindergarten rendition."

"Think code breaker. Super smart, number-theory kind of shit. If she had a lock, you wouldn't be able to get inside unless she wanted you to."

I whistled low. "So, chances are she has a lock somewhere someone wants to pick?"

Ariel shrugged. "I don't know yet." She pulled up another file. "This one is the file on Willa MacKenzie. She was an art dealer and the reason for all that loot little Mayzie has come in to. Some of her clients have been... let's just say questionable. We probably start here."

I frowned. "Why don't we hit all the angles. Pretty boy can take the boyfriend. You pull double duty with your superior hacker skills to figure out who from Willa's past might think they have something coming to them. I'll take Neela and the kid and poke around the house. I'll have access. She told me she's moving the company to the guesthouse on the property, so everyone will be contained."

Ariel lifted a brow, and I had to remind myself to keep my comments to myself. I needed this gig. And as much as it rankled, I was not in charge here. Trace also gave me a questioning look.

Ariel's smile was beatific, but it didn't fool me for a second. "You're the expert now?"

"I'm just saying. The eejit who grabbed her kept asking for *it*. Something specific. We can't rule any threats out at this point."

"Lucky for you, you're right. And if you'd let me finish, I would have made the assignments."

Fuck. "Sorry. Used to being on my own."

Trace eyed me. "Not a team player then?"

I ignored him. I needed to remember why I was here. The mermaid princess currently held my future in her hands. I needed to chill. "Sorry."

Ariel studied me. "You okay with the client? You want the newbie to take her?"

The fuck I did. "Nah, I'm good. Besides, the kid has already fallen for my charm."

Trace snorted then. "That's only because she hasn't met me yet."

Ariel rolled her eyes. "I'm going to do a little tunneling for dirt. See if anything suspicious comes up."

I nodded. "So basic shift rotation."

She nodded. "That's the eventual plan. I've got two more leads I need to chase down. For now, Trace, you'll be on research for the next day or so. I'll do what I can from the road."

I sat back in the conference chair and double-checked the monitor. Neela, *Ms. Wellbrook* I reminded myself, was safe at home behind her very heavy walls and very hard gates. Ariel and I had needed to touch base before I went in. I figured she was safe at home, but I was still anxious to check on her. Seeing that piece of shit with his hand over her mouth... Well, I hadn't been that angry in a long time.

I needed to get back to her.

You need to get your shit together.

"Keep things super low profile. I'll create you a background to match, but I'll keep the details close to the truth in case there are any slip-ups. Are you up for this assignment?"

"Yeah, sure." I'd agree to anything that would get me back to her.

She grinned then. "I think it'll be easier if you're on premises full time."

I sat up straighter. "What?" I was toast if I had to live with her round the clock.

"We don't have the manpower to swap out yet. I can't have Trace relieve you every 12 hours until I'm back. You're scheduled for a full day with the kid then off, but I think we should suggest you be full-time with occasional replacements."

"Yeah it's fine. Let's deal with the immediate threat, then we'll figure it out."

"Well then, looks like we are official. Okay, grab your gear and head over to the house. See you in a couple of days."

"Roger that."

As we walked out, I heard Trace mutter under his breath, "Is there a reason you don't want to stay with the client?"

"Nope, it's all good."

Lies. All lies.

Chapter *eight*

NEELA

I stared at the book. I didn't even want to open it. I didn't know what secrets I would find there.

At the end of the day, I needed something to distract me so I wouldn't keep staring out the window, waiting for the boogeyman to jump out and go, "Booga-booga!"

Though the boogeyman would certainly not say that. He'd probably say, "I'm going to carry you off and rape and kill you now."

I ran my hands through my hair, gathering the thick length of it and knotting it on top of my head.

Okay, first things first. I looked at Mayzie who was banging things on her playpen.

"It's really simple being a baby, isn't it?"

She just gurgled and spit and banged her blocks.

"Right. Of course, you would say that. What I'm saying is, I have to try and figure out what your mommy left me."

She was also helpful and muttered. "Ma."

"Yeah, your mommy. Okay, first things first, a good code cracker needs their fuel." I reached inside my purse and pulled out a bag of peanut M&Ms. I took note that my hands were still shaking. Clearly, the adrenaline had maxed out.

It was fine. I was fine. Everything was fine. Never mind that the police had spoken to me about some asshole trying to grab me off the street. Or rather, Mayzie. He wanted me to give him Mayzie, of all things. As if. "Okay, maybe your mama left a clue as to why somebody wants to get you and this."

I held up the book. Mayzie seemed uninterested.

I had my peanut M&Ms, but that wasn't enough for the task at hand. "Also, I need caffeine."

Unfortunately, when I marched into the kitchen and opened the fridge, I remembered I hadn't bought anything. And all Willa had in there were those tasteless carbonated water things.

Yup. For this, I was going to need sugar. I knew sugar wasn't great for me, but I was a sugar addict. I worked out, tried to eat right for the most part, but I needed my colas, sodas, anything really. It helped fuel the brain.

I finally found something way in the back, some kind of a juice soda. It would have to do.

When I returned, Mayzie was standing up in her playpen. She'd dropped one of the green blocks out of it, and she was trying to reach for it, except she had very short, chubby hands.

When I grabbed it for her, she rewarded me with a mostly toothless grin. And all right, maybe she was the devil's spawn, but her little grin was everything.

Don't tell me you like the baby.

As babies went, she was okay. Golden curls, bright green eyes, chubby little hands with dimples on the knuckles. Yeah, as babies went, she was okay, if you were into that sort of thing.

Well, you better like that sort of thing. She's yours now.

I tried not to think about that. I had to focus on the damn book.

I also reached into my bag for my inspection gloves. I usually use them for things like first edition books, and yes, I was nerdy enough to have my own pair. But sometimes when people wanted me to crack something, it was best if I didn't physically touch it. The hands secreted oils on everything. And to crack a code, I liked to keep things pristine.

I also pulled out a clear plastic bag to store the journal in temporarily.

I sat cross-legged on the couch and cracked it open. Symbols, nothing but symbols. Symbols I couldn't understand. A lot of cryptanalysts like to start with a computer, but I was old school.

My father taught me to always look for the patterns. There are patterns in everything. Mother Nature doesn't make any mistakes. And when someone is trying to hide something, as complicated as they try to make it sound, they always use a pattern.

I smiled at that. This journal was clearly handwritten, so that meant, somewhere in there, amongst the symbols and triangles and squiggly lines, there was some kind of pattern. There were some odd spaces in between the lines, but I couldn't quite make out their purpose.

I looked at what I thought was the front. Something that looked like a *fleur de lis* was sketched on it.

But what the fuck does it mean?

I had no idea.

"Come on, Neela, start with what you know."

I pulled open my laptop and went through my step-by-step process. When dealing with languages, it's best to start with the known, and then with the ancients, and then try and extrapolate from that information what code someone might be using.

I had seen people use Latin, ancient Aramaic, Sanskrit, even Austrian. I had seen a lot of things.

But my father was right, people always used patterns.

Ten minutes of digging, told me that this oh-so-easy language to decode, was not that easy. It told me that the language in this journal was neither Sanskrit, Austrian, or Latin, although, I knew that one, or any Roman language. Again, not a surprise. It was also not ancient Aramaic or hieroglyphs.

Okay, then. It wasn't Russian. It wasn't Eastern. At least, not any Eastern that was in my repertoire. I leaned forward and stared at it. "What are you?"

Mayzie dragged me out of my reverie when she started to hiccup repeatedly.

I glanced up and her face was scrunched. "No, no, no, no. You are not going to cry. You're not going to cry."

But she was too far gone. *Hiccup! Hiccup! Hiccup!* And *Whaaaaa!*

I quickly closed the journal and ran to pick her up. As I held her in my arms, I tried to lay her head on my chest, but she bucked back. "Jesus Christ, you need to stop that. I almost dropped you."

That only made her scream more.

"Listen kid, you've got to start talking to me. At what age do you guys start talking?"

It was clear to the both of us that I was terrible at this. I glanced longingly back at that journal.

It would have to wait until Mayzie was asleep, because clearly, I wasn't going to get any work done on it right now. "What in the world did you give me, Willa? And why me, of all people?"

PENNY

Something was wrong with my husband.

He'd been silent and broody through dinner. And he had canceled game night. It had been a busy few weeks, and I hadn't been able to see Ariel since she'd walked out.

And canceling game night meant I definitely wasn't going to see her. I could just grab a Guard and go down to her, but I knew she'd been out of town.

"So, is now a good time to ask you what's wrong?"

Sebastian pulled me close and ran a hand down my arm. "Nothing."

"That's bullshit. You've been silent and distant. What's going on?"

It took a moment, then he sighed. "The incident in Austria… They were targeting my cousin."

My eyes went wide. "What?"

"We've managed to keep it out of the news, but that's what's going on."

"Holy shit." Sebastian's cousin, Tristan, was one of his cousins that I actually *did* like.

"The Council thinks the whole family is tainted. All my cousins, Uncle Roland, even though Roland abdicated the throne. None of them have been home basically since Ashton was exiled.

"Look, Tristan has a career. He's an international soccer star. Him not coming home might not have anything to do with any self-imposed exile."

He raised his brow. "And Alix? Is there a reason she hasn't been home?"

I sighed. "Look, Ashton was a terror. He tortured a lot of people, including his own siblings. So maybe they're not real anxious to return home. But outside of that, I can't believe that we deliberately wouldn't send them more aid."

He shook his head. "The Council won't approve it. And that's that. Roone, ever so helpful, already suggested that I send Ariel, and I would, except she's civilian now. So, I can't."

I cursed under my breath. "Stupid fucking rules. She would have been perfect."

"Yeah, I know."

I turned into his hold and dropped my purse with my phone and all my notes in it. "Is there anything I could do to make you feel better?"

True to form, his gaze narrowed, and his pupils dilated. "I still have to solve the problem, but maybe a kiss from my wife would soothe the rough edges."

I laughed. "Sebastian, we're having a serious conversation here."

He started backing me up. I wasn't sure exactly where we were heading, but I knew that probably in less than a minute, he'd be inside me. "I can have a serious conversation while I'm making love to my wife."

"No, you cannot. Because I know how the blood that's supposed to be used for brain cells will be used for another task entirely."

"I can do both."

When my back hit the wall, I sighed. Lately, he hadn't been exactly keen on talking to me. Making love to me, absolutely. But *talking*, not really. It was like he was using sex as a balm for all the pressure he'd been under.

He was putting all his energy into the things that were going right, which was fine, except, he needed to *talk* about the other stuff... eventually. "Seb, I'm serious. Let me at least try to figure out how to help you. Maybe we can hire someone on the sly. Oh, maybe even Blake Security. They are good with keeping things quiet."

He shook his head. "It was one thing when my father was alive, before the conspiracy. Blake Security has protected me more than once. But now the Council is sticking by the letter of the law. I can try and force their hands, but that will take time. And I'm not the diplomat you are. I just hate every minute of it. I am the bloody king. I should have the final say."

"That is not how our laws work, love. You know that."

He leaned close. "Right now, I feel hindered because I can't do anything to protect my cousin. He wasn't part of any of this. He was just minding his business. But right now, he could be in danger."

"Look, we'll figure it out."

He nodded even as he dragged his teeth over his bottom lip. I knew that look. He needed to blow off steam, and no amount of talking was going to bring him down off the tightwire.

"What is it you need Sebastian? Tell me what you need, and I'll give it to you."

He cupped both my hands in one of his and raised my arms high over my head. "Right now, I need my wife."

"Sex isn't really an answer, my love."

He chuckled then. It was so nice to see that smile. I'd been missing it. "No, but it is the question." Easily, he pressed his hand on my hip, turning me around so I faced the wall. He gently squeezed my wrists and leaned down to whisper in my ear. "Keep these here."

There was no point in trying to talk to him now, because his brain was already in my pants, doing all sorts of delicious things. Not that I was complaining. But I wanted him to open up and just share things with me to find solutions together. I knew the pressure he was under. I knew he was terrified of messing up.

But he should have been happier. Lucas and Jessa were home. Safe. But instead, he was even more stressed out.

Both his hands were on the slick buckle of my pants. No question. No preamble. He leaned in and kissed my neck, nipping gently. My pants were unbuttoned and sliding down my feet in seconds. My panties came next, and then his fingers were in the juncture of my thighs. "Open up."

"Sebastian." I drew in a shuddering breath. It wasn't fair. I had a plan. But now his fingers were on me and I couldn't think. I couldn't breathe. I just wanted him inside me. I wondered maybe if I could give him a couple of orgasms, he would relax enough to be able to talk to me. Also, I wanted an orgasm now, so there was that.

"Wider, Len." The use of my nickname was a stroke of electricity twisting around my spine. When I had gone undercover, that was the name I used, Len. He only used it now when he was so turned on he couldn't wait.

"S-seb—"

"Yeah?"

"Hurry."

I could feel his smile against my neck. His fingers didn't bother with the buttons on my blouse. He just yanked it open in the front and then peeled it off of one shoulder so he could have better access to my neck.

He nipped the bone at the top of my shoulder and nuzzled into my neck. Before I knew it, he was lifting me gently and then he was sliding home.

I gasped at the fullness. "Jesus."

His groan was more of a growl into my skin. "Yes. Just what I needed."

"Sebastian, God."

When he started to move, I promptly forgot why I would ever want to talk. Talking was overrated. This was so much better for connection and communication anyway.

As I spiraled toward bliss, the little voice inside my head was screaming.

You are in a sex fog. Snap out of it. He needs to talk.

Okay. Okay. We'd talk later. Post orgasm. I just—I needed one.

He picked up his speed, and I tried to stay upright on my shoes. His hands slipped up my belly, cupping my breasts. He growled in my ear. "You're so fucking tight."

"You're so big… hurry."

It didn't take long. Before I knew what was happening, my body started to quiver, pulsing around him. He chuckled as he nipped my ear. "That's my queen. Always so eager. So ready. I will always need this."

And then I was coming, a triggered explosion going off in my body. Hard. Fast, like I'd been hit by a truck. And he wasn't far behind me. His little growl vibrated in my ear as he panted and held me upright, locking himself inside me.

"Jesus, woman."

"Me? I was just standing here minding my own business."

I could tell he was shaking his head. He moved my curls off the nape of my neck and planted a kiss. "Nope. This is all you. I was completely fine until you started talking to me and asking me how you could take my mind off of things. Congratulations, I am now incapable of thought."

"Yeah, I'm incapable of thought too. Thanks for that."

He chuckled low. "Okay, we'll try thought in a few minutes. And then we'll see if I'm still inside you when we try to have those thoughts."

"No. We're supposed to talk."

He shook his head, kissing the nape of my neck again. "We talk a lot. Right now, I don't think I need to talk anymore."

"Okay. We'll just stand here resting for a minute." The only thing was I could still feel him inside me. Hot. Hard. Thick.

"Jesus, Sebastian, how can you go again?"

"I'm not saying I can go again. I'm just saying I'm already here, so it's comfy. And warm. And tight. Like a hug for my dick."

"More impossible."

"So my queen says."

I don't know what it was about the way he said my queen, but it had me thinking of all the courts, the old European courts, and in my mind, I saw a coat of armor. I turned my neck. "Sebastian?"

"Yes, sweetheart?"

"What about knights?"

"What?"

"Knights, like Sir Lancelot. That makes you King Arthur. You could get a round table."

"Are you sure we should redecorate right now?"

I laughed, and it did the most delicious things to exactly where he was lodged inside me. He groaned low. "Jesus, woman."

"Sorry, you're the one who's still inside me, but what I'm saying is *knights*. I know that the Royal Guard are essentially knights, but not really. Is there anything in the bylaws that say you can't have a legion of knights? From what I remember in history, there were knights before. We just eventually combined them into Royal Guard."

He stopped laughing for a moment. "Oh my God, you might be right."

I smiled. "What you don't seem to understand is that I'm always right."

He nipped my nape, and it was my turn to shudder again. "Careful, woman."

"Who needs to be careful? When you're right as much as I am, you can pretty much say whatever wild thing comes to your brain."

He nipped me again. "You are a fucking genius."

"I know. So, when you hire Lancelot, I promise I won't let him fall in love with me."

He laughed then. "That's kind of impossible. As beautiful as you are, and smart, you're basically the whole package."

"You flatter me. You just want to be inside my pants."

"I'm already inside your pants."

I laughed then. And there was that delicious feeling again. I could feel him harden and twitch. "I told you about that. Now look what you've done. Now what are you going to do about it?"

With a chuckle, he slid his hand down my belly, parting my lips and slid his fingers through my soft skin. "That was not my fault."

"Sure, it was. Now for your punishment, I'm going to eat you up."

"Do you promise?"

"Oh, I promise."

Maybe talking *was* overrated.

Chapter
nine

NEELA

I was entirely too happy to see Jax on my doorstep late that afternoon. "You're here."

I was clearly a master at small talk.

"I'm here."

He had only a small duffle with him. I swallowed my disappointment. It's not like the man was really moving in with me. He was here to look after Mayzie. "Let me show you to the other guest cottage. It's fully stocked with whatever you might need. I checked myself today. It has its own private plunge pool too, but of course you're more than—"

He cut me off. "Ms. Wellbrook?"

Geez the way he said that, his accent nearly reduced me to mush. "Call me Neela. You saved my life. You've earned the right."

"Okay, Neela. Thank you for the guest cottage, but it's better that I'm in the main house as close to the baby as possible. If I stay in the guest house, I certainly won't hear Mayzie crying."

My brows drew down. "Oh shit. I guess I didn't think about that. Clearly I have no experience with babies or nannies."

His smile was gentle. "You've had a bit on your mind. How are you feeling? How is Mayzie?"

I was still a little numb from earlier, but I didn't want to get into it. "I'm fine. Mayzie took a nap for the first time this afternoon after we came back, so I think she had a bit of a scare too."

The muscle in his jaw flexed. "I'm sorry about that. What can I do to make things better for you?"

Libido: *Orgasms would certainly relax me.*

Nope. Not on offer.

"I'm good. Thank you for asking."

Libido: *The hell we're good. We're in danger of atrophy over here. He knows how to fix us.*

The way those azure-blue depths stared into mine, I was inclined to believe it.

Upstairs, Mayzie wailed, and I sighed. I made for the stairs, but he stopped me. "I'll get her. You take a load off. I'll bring her down. It's almost 5:30. She has to be hungry."

"You'd think. But she refuses to eat for me."

"We'll see if we can't fix that."

I won't say I didn't enjoy the view. I was in the kitchen trying to make something for Mayzie when he returned. Mayzie had tears in her eyes, but she was quietly sucking her thumb.

"She okay?" I was itching to reach out and take her, but I knew that was likely to add to her tears. We still hadn't gotten used to each other yet. Even though she seemed perfectly happy with him.

Just how bad was I at this mothering thing that she was happier with a stranger?

Jax wasted no time; he just marched over to me and handed me Mayzie. "You take her. I'll do that."

Flustered, I stumbled over my words. I wasn't used to someone telling me what to do. "Oh, it's okay. I'm almost done. Getting her to eat is a major pain."

He took one sniff of the organic pea-and-carrot concoction from the super, hyped-up, all-natural mom brand and frowned. "No wonder she won't eat. Even this organic stuff comes with a smell. It's the packaging. I don't know why, but my niece was the same way. She wouldn't eat a single flavor of the stuff. But if we made her food ourselves, she'd gobble it right up."

I blinked. "What?"

He slid a glance at Mayzie, who was still slapping her hands on my cheeks.

"I'm here. Let me help. Me. The *manny*."

"Do you know you wrinkle your nose every time you say the word manny?"

He scrubbed a knuckle over the edge of his nose. It was cute. "I prefer child minder or child care provider."

I grinned. "I think manny is cute."

What? No. No. *Not* cute manny.

God, how long had it been since I'd had an orgasm? Though that question was neither here nor there because I was not shagging the new manny. Because that is not something that I did. I played it safe for obvious reasons, because if I didn't, the world would turn to shit.

"How do you even know what to do with kids? I feel like I'm fumbling around in the dark with a blindfold on and someone is blasting death metal all the time."

"I told you, I have a niece. I used to watch her a lot. They moved to Sweden, but they used to live on the big island, and I'd see her every week. I also have eight nephews scattered around the world."

Watching him talk about his niece, I could see his face soften. His hard edges were gone. He was still strikingly beautiful. But less like the lethal edge of a sword and more like insanely hot role model. I wasn't sure which I preferred.

"I just—" I took a deep breath to get my emotions under control. "I don't know what to do."

He indicated the seat at the island. " You sit there, and I'll pull some stuff out of the fridge. Were you able to go shopping yet?"

I shook my head. "I've been ordering food every day, which makes me just feel gross."

"Hey, it's a way to get things done. Don't feel bad about actually finding a way through the chaos."

"Yeah, I want to do it right with Mayzie. Every perfect mom in a magazine says do it right, but I'm overwhelmed if I'm being honest. I never planned on having a kid on my own, you know? And my plate was pretty full already, so it's just been a little much."

"No problem. You sit. Make a list of the things that you need. Or at least know that you need, or think that you need, or have always wanted."

"Yeah? Then what?"

He pulled vegetables out of the fridge. Spinach and broccoli, and then the white sweet potatoes that I had. I didn't like the orange ones when I made fries. It just looked weird.

"Do you have any apples? Or applesauce?"

"Yes, I have applesauce. Or at least there's some in the pantry. I didn't know if she was old enough for it or not."

"Yeah, I think she is. But when in doubt, Google it."

He typed something quickly into his phone and then he nodded. "Yes, she can have applesauce." And then he searched in the freezer and found some peas.

"You make your list. I'll make her something she'll eat."

"Something she'll eat?"

He shrugged. "I certainly hope so. Or you and I will be eating this concoction for dinner."

My stomach grumbled. "Oh my God. I should feed you, right? I should totally feed you."

He shook his head and held up his hand. "You, sit. I can feed myself, and you look like you need someone to do something for you for once. So, it'll be simple, but I can manage."

"Seriously, where did you come from?"

He grinned. "The Islands, by way of London."

"That sounds like a fascinating story."

He shrugged. "Not really. List."

"Um, I don't even know what to write down."

"Just say it out loud, make the note, and then you and I will figure out how we're going to get it done."

"I swear you're like a buff Mary Poppins."

He paused as he grabbed the chopping board from the cupboard. "So, you think I'm buff?"

"Now I also think you're cocky."

He chuckled then. "Make your list."

"I still need to go through all the paperwork. There is so much to deal with in terms of the gallery."

"I get it. What about your assistants? Do you trust them to do the business things?"

She nodded. "Implicitly. They handle my business, but I don't know if they can handle something additional."

"All right, you probably need to hire someone else. But for now, pull one of them into taking care of stuff at Willa's gallery. At least temporarily."

He had a point there. "Yeah, that's probably a good idea. I

guess I can add that to the list. What, you're going to take over my life and make everything perfect for me?"

It was a joke. I swear to God it was a joke. But he turned, and the look he gave me was so intense I swear the man could see my uterus contracting. "You've hired Royal Elite. It's part of the service. Anything you need, I'll provide."

Libido: *See earlier note about orgasms.*

I bit my bottom lip before I could respond. But my skin went hot and prickly. Could he see? I was a native islander, so I'd been all mixed up with my Afro-Caribbean heritage, some East Indian, some Caucasian, and it left me with a bronze complexion, that made it hard to identify me ethnically. It also made it hard to see when I was going red. "I'll keep that in mind."

Those eyes of his, the way they assessed me, fluttered over my body for the briefest moment before flickering back to my eyes. "Good."

Jesus Christ. I felt like he'd just licked me all over. And if he licked me, was I his now?

Hell yes.

"I have to take Mayzie to her doctor's appointment tomorrow morning."

"Okay, we'll all go. Remember, you're not going anywhere without me now."

"Oh my God, it's like you're married to me now."

He shot me a grin over his shoulder as he chopped up the sweet potato. "You don't seem so bad. Besides, we're already intimately acquainted. And I like how you fight. I almost let you pummel the arsehole. It brought fire to your eyes. It was a little scary, but also sort of brilliant."

Oh boy. I was going to need a change of underwear. The man was good with the kid, concocting something she might eat, and liked me with fire in my eyes. Was there a hot-guy factory that would have made more of him? Because obviously, I couldn't bang my manny. But I could bang one *just* like him if there was a copy.

"Um, thank you, I guess."

"What else do you need? Seriously. When I say that, I mean it. I'll take care of everything you need."

"If you can fix my love life too, I might have to marry you."

He lifted a brow. "Trouble in paradise? Is there anyone I need to kill?"

Why was that really hot? "No. Just my ex. It's fine now He's not worth thinking about. I just have to rebuild everything thanks to him. It's like he deliberately wanted to tear me down. What kind of guy does that?"

"Let me be clear with you. That's not a real man. A real man would celebrate your successes, encourage you, and want you to succeed if it made you happy. He was a twat."

I slid a glance at the baby.

He shook his head. "She doesn't know what that means yet, but I will watch my language with her."

"Okay. So yeah, those are the parts of my life I need to fix, and if you could possibly bring Willa back from the dead, that would be amazing."

"Well, I don't know how to do that. But the other things I can sort of make happen. What about staff? Who do you want in the house?"

"Uh, I don't need staff."

"Sure you do. This is a really big house and it's going to need to be dusted. Little miss over there, is mobile. She will put just about anything into her mouth. While you are trying to protect her, she's actually trying to kill herself, so you need someone to clean."

"Oh, right. Okay, um, I guess I'll need a cleaning service?"

He nodded. "I'll get someone to come once a week."

"Just like that? You're like a fairy godfather."

"As long as you need me, I'll be here."

"Just like Mary Poppins."

He flashed a grin. "I'm better looking than Mary Poppins."

"Fair enough. A buff Mary Poppins." Shit. I covered my face with my hands. "Can we just forget that I said that, *again?*"

"Well, maybe I don't want to forget that you said that."

"Um, it's just—you, uh, I guess you're working for me now, so let's just pretend I'm professional."

He chuckled then. "It's forgotten. Besides, you should probably be more worried about the part where you grabbed my dick."

My mouth fell open as heat flushed my body. "Oh my God, I grabbed your belt."

"I mean, your mouth was like an inch from it. So, you were basically grabbing my dick."

I covered my face. "Oh my God, I'm going to die."

He chuckled. "You know what else I'm going to work on? Loosening you up so you don't take everything so seriously. I'm teasing you. Everything is forgotten. Strictly professional."

"Exactly."

Lies. All lies.

ARIEL

For some reason, it was easier to talk to Tamsin than it was to talk with the men. She wasn't immediately distrustful.

Trace hadn't been distrustful exactly, but it was clear he wasn't exactly sure about working for me until I used Lucas's name.

"Wait, so you have your own shop?" Tamsin seemed either a little incredulous or impressed. Maybe both.

"Yeah. I just started it. It's small, and we are hustling for clients, but we already have some on the roster. I need a team, and I need to build one fast. You always had a great reputation in the academy. And you had exemplary military service. Honestly, I'm surprised you didn't go into the Royal Guard."

Tamsin shook her head. "Yeah, well, when you make the mistake of dating your commanding officer and find out he's going in the Royal Guard, it kind of sours you on the whole *for king and country* thing. So, I went into the private sector."

"Okay, so what's it gonna take to woo you away from your current employer?"

Tamsin sat back and fiddled with her drink. I was already here when she arrived, sitting in the far corner. I'd watched her as she ordered a seltzer water with lime. But to anyone else watching, it would have looked like a gin and tonic or something. She appeared to be cool and relaxed, completely in control of all her faculties, which I appreciated. "Do I get to set my own hours?"

"Not entirely, but we can work around that."

Tamsin nodded. "If I say I don't want to work with a client, is that gonna be a problem?"

"Well, I will ask you why. I want to know if a client is abusive or harassing any of my team members."

She nodded. "Thank you."

I lifted a brow. "Has that been a problem at your current place?"

"Let's just say that sometimes the people you're protecting don't know that your only job is protect them not anything else."

I ground my teeth. "No. Not on my watch."

"Do you have any particular rules?"

"Um, I think there is only one, or maybe two really. One,

don't date the clients. That'll look bad."

"Of course. Trust me, I mixed business and pleasure once. I will never do that again."

I winced. "Ended badly?"

"That's an understatement."

"Okay. The second one is just team dinners on the last Sunday of the month. I think it's important, team bonding and all that."

Tamsin nodded slowly. "Sure, as long as no one's a dick that shouldn't be a problem."

I laughed. "Well, the guys are actually pretty cool. Don't tell them I said that, though. I like to bust Jax's chops. He's British, hot, and he knows it. But he's a good soldier. He knows what he wants. And considering who referred him, he's solid. I know I can trust him with my life, and I haven't even known him that long. Trace is coming back home, and he's in charge of his kid sister, so he has his own reasons for what he's doing. And he's also a good-looking son of a bitch, but he's cool. More relaxed, less intense than Jax, but good at his job. I have a strict no assholes policy. If anyone's an asshole, they get booted. Sound good?"

Tamsin nodded. "Yes, that sounds pretty good to me. And it would be nice to work with a woman for a change."

"Yeah, down with the patriarchy and all that. But honestly, if you have a problem, you just need to talk to me. We'll figure this out as we go. I thought I'd be Guard my whole life, you know?"

Tamsin nodded in solidarity. "That was my path. That was where I was going to go." She shrugged. "Plans change. And now, they're changing for the better I think."

I grinned at her. My phone buzzed on the table, and I scowled at it. No one even had my new number except for Trace and Jax, and Penny and Sebastian, of course. I'd changed my number after the whole *my dad was a traitor* thing. The only people that needed to reach me were the palace, Penny, and my team anyway. I'd whittled down on the outside friends since when you're a traitor's daughter, everyone has something to say about it. "I am so sorry. It might be one of the team."

Tamsin waved a hand. "Stop, it's fine." When I turned it over and saw who was calling, the bottom fell out of my stomach. "I'll be right back."

I left her at the bar and marched to the far corner where I'd previously been seated and no one could overhear me. "Hello. Sebastian? What's wrong? Is Penny okay?"

The king paused for a moment. "Yeah. Why would you ask that?"

"Well, you don't usually call me unless there's a problem."

"Yes, I do."

I groaned. "Oh my God, what do you want?"

"I do call you."

"No, you wait until Penny calls me then you grab the phone from her and chat with me for a minute, and then you hand the phone back to Penny. You never actually *call* yourself."

"Well, I've called you now."

I rolled my eyes. "Okay, what do you need?"

"I do resent the fact that you think I'm calling because I need something."

"Well, don't you need something?"

"Yeah. Actually, it's a little sensitive. Do you mind coming out to the palace? There's something I want you to take a look at."

"You're freaking me out. Do we still have assassins on our ass? Because last time you had a special job for me, we got shot at. All of us."

"No, I don't think it's something like that. I don't know. I just want you to look into it for me. Can you come to the palace?"

"Actually, I'm not in the islands at the moment. I'm on a different set of islands entirely. Can I come up tomorrow? I fly back tonight."

I could hear the frown in his voice. "Where are you?"

"Well, when the prince sends you a file of someone to recruit, you do as you're told."

I could almost hear him relax. "Oh, you found Tamsin."

"Yes, Your Majesty. And, I think she's perfect."

"Good, I always liked her. I never knew why she didn't join the Royal Guard, and Lucas and I figured she'd make a great addition to your team."

"Yeah, I think she's perfect."

"Great. So, I'll see you tomorrow?"

"Yeah, I'll text you when I land and see what time works."

"Perfect. See you tomorrow."

"Okay. Give Penny a kiss for me."

He chuckled low. "I'll do a lot more than that."

"Ew. Do you have to say shit like that? My God, the two of you, I'll tell you right now, get a room."

He laughed then. "I have a whole palace."

"Jesus Christ. I'll see you tomorrow." And then I hung up on the king. I glared at the phone for a long moment. I probably shouldn't have hung up on the king, but who cares? By that point, Sebastian had taken on big brother status with me, so I figured I could hang up on him.

As I returned to the table, I tried not to let my mind spin about what he needed to see me about. Whatever it was, I could handle it. In the meantime, I had a new teammate. And I needed to lock that in. Something told me I was going to be very busy going forward.

Chapter ten

NEELA

This was a mistake. What else could it be?

The hottest man I'd ever seen in my life, was living under my roof now, which was less than ideal.

And of course, Mayzie adored him. Even from upstairs, I could hear her squealing and giggling. The little traitor had loved his concoction of white sweet potatoes and peas and apple sauce. She'd tucked in as if she'd been starving for days.

To make matters worse, the man could cook. He pulled out some chicken, taken those same potatoes and seasoning, and put together something that smelled insanely delicious. Even upstairs, where he'd sent me to have a long hot bath, I could smell it.

A bath.

When was the last time I'd had a bath?

My old flat didn't have a bathtub, but there was an insanely deep, giant soaking tub at Willa's.

He told me it would take 45 minutes for dinner to be ready. That was enough time to soak, wasn't it?

I stared at the tub and couldn't help myself. I turned on the water. I tossed in some bubble bath really quickly. I wouldn't have time to completely fill it, but there would be a good amount of water in there, even if I only got to soak for ten minutes.

I quickly undressed and piled my hair up high. I'd straightened it yesterday, so if I got it all wet, the curls would divert back. And they wouldn't be cute springy curls. They would be fuzzy and all over the place.

I needed to get it together. A needed a set of rules to remember why I could *not* shag my new nanny. He worked for me, and it would feel like I was paying for sex.

He probably didn't want to sleep with me anyway. Never mind those stares that make me feel like he was looking at me naked.

He was there to take care of Mayzie, and I need that more than I need an orgasm.

Nope. We would argue you need a lot more.

I shoved my libido out of the conversation. It had been so, so long since I'd had satisfying sex. Hell, since someone had even touched me in a sexual way.

Something told me my new nanny knew how to go down. But I really needed to stop because it wasn't going to happen.

I picked up my phone that I'd left at the edge of tub and texted Bex.

Neela: *SOS. I need you to help me not bang my new manny.*

Bex: *You mean the hot guy with the incredible eyes and the body that says 'Hi, I know how to fuck?'*

Me: *Yes.*

Bex: *I'm sorry. I can't get behind this plan. I think you should fuck him.*

Me: *Bex, are you serious? I need him for Mayzie.*

Bex: *I would argue that your orgasms are just as necessary as Mayzie's happiness. I vote shag him to bits.*

Me: *I'm not shagging him.*

Adam: *Yes, I vote for shag as well. Although, why am I included in this conversation?*

My face flamed.

I'd forgotten that when I typed in SOS, it automatically added *both* of them to the message. It was a feature I'd asked for within our messaging app.

Me: *Damn it. Sorry Adam.*

Adam: *No problem. But look, I'm straight, and even I know that dude is hot. I felt very insecure just being in his presence.*

I snorted a laugh. Adam was gorgeous. Sandy blonde hair, chocolatey brown eyes, a smile that was quick and roguish. Girls loved him. When I had female clients, no matter the age, I took him along. He worked it for our benefit, which meant *my* benefit. It also helped that he was dangerously smart, and from what I had seen at a beach day we'd all had together, he had a hell of a six pack.

Me: *I'm pretty sure you feel secure enough.*

Adam: *Nope. The guy is huge.*

I snorted to myself again and typed out: 'That's what she—' and then I started deleting it. I was their boss. I couldn't say things like that. That's what I had Bex for.

Bex: *That's what she said.*

And then she admonished me.

Bex: *I swear to God, Neela, you're slipping.*

Me: *You guys are no help.*

Adam: *So, what's the consensus? Are we shagging him?*

Me: *I'm getting off the phone now.*

Bex: *Smiley face.*

Adam: *She's getting off the phone now, so she can go shag him.*

I groaned and slipped further in the water, the warmth lapping at my tight muscles. I absolutely, positively was not going to shag the manny.

You just keep telling yourself that.

I had to. Because until I got my life in order, shagging someone who worked for me was out of the question.

Chapter eleven

NEELA

What was I missing?

I'd been through this journal over and over again.

These symbols meant something, the way they were organized, certain symbol combinations on the left, other symbols located on the right. It was in a diary of some sort. But it didn't look like it was in a fluid style of writing.

What are you?

Or maybe it was nothing at all, and Willa was just fucking with me. It was classic Willa. She'd have loved the idea of me spinning out over a puzzle. She'd have loved to give me some nonsense just to make me squirm.

But why leave it to me, the one person who would obsess over it forever?

I felt rather than heard Jax in the doorway, his nearness making my hair stand on end. When I glanced up, he had a mug in his hand. "You were concentrating so hard I didn't want to disturb you."

I shook my head. "Sorry, were you asking me something?"

He shook his head as he chuckled. "No. I just brought you tea."

Tea? He'd brought me tea. Great. Just when I'd convinced myself that going anywhere near him was a terrible, very bad, no-good idea, he was being sweet. Which was possibly even more difficult to shake off than the tight quarters with a sex god who was so hot he could burn layers of skin off. "Um, thank you. You didn't have to do that."

He shook his head. "I know. But you've been holed up in the library so long I figured you might need sustenance. I even included a digestive or two. The chocolate ones."

I blinked at him. "Digestives?"

He shrugged. "You know, they're a British cookie, I guess? I never know which ones I'll find on the island."

I sighed and put the journal down. I took my glasses off then rubbed my eyes. "Thank you. I've just been kind of diving headfirst into this journal thing, and I can't figure it out, so it's making me crazy."

"What is that?"

"When Willa died, she left me this journal. The problem is I can't read it, and I have no idea what it means."

Jax frowned. "Do you mind if I take a look?"

I laughed. "Be my guest." I handed it over to him, our fingers lightly brushing in the transfer. I snatched mine back quickly, hoping he didn't notice the zing of electricity that furled its way into my bloodstream, heating me, making me want more of that kind of touch.

Nope. Not going to happen.

Jax frowned as he stared at the journal. "I have no idea what these symbols are."

"Join the club. At first, I thought they were maybe some take on a fluid artistic language like, Arabic or Samarian, but it's not. I checked. None of those symbols are familiar. I have a program I ran them through, and it should at least tell me the language so I'd know where to look, but it's not recognizable. And you know, taking a closer look, the styling is different. It's certainly not Eastern. It's not related to Chinese, or Japanese, or Korean, and I can't pinpoint what it is. I just... ugh! The frustration. And it's not even as if I can't just pinpoint the swirl in these symbols over here, but then there are also these block symbols, as if they're part of some symbolic computer language or something. I don't know. The mixing of the two is just really throwing me off. Fuck if I know."

He chuckled and it sounded like a low rumble. "I don't think I've heard you swear before."

I flushed. "I'm trying really hard for the baby. With my luck, her first word would be fuck."

He grinned. "Didn't know you had it in you."

"Oh, I have it in me. It just depends on how pissed off I get."

"How do you do that anyway? Decode a language?"

I took the journal back as he offered it. "I mean there's all this number theory that goes into it, but I just like puzzles. I'm not a natural or anything, but my brain won't ever let one go. Honestly, I'm just one of those people who can't leave something unsolved. I *have* to figure things out. The human brain is fascinating. Sometimes I leave something alone for weeks, or months, or a couple of years, and then my brain will magically just unlock it for me, and I can go back and solve whatever it was I couldn't solve before."

"And you do that for work? Computer programs?"

I nodded. "For work, I do all the boring number theory stuff because I don't have the luxury of being precious about the puzzle muse. Most of my biggest clients are governments or video game builders. My company was built on the backs of video game companies, all trying to outdo each other, create the unwinnable game or the uncrackable code, and they hire people like me to do just that or to build it for them. Something so insanely encrypted no one can get past it, except for the very, very few."

"That's amazing. I don't think I ever even solved a Rubix cube."

Lie.

I didn't know how I knew. It was more than a feeling though. He was lying. I don't know *how* I knew, but I did. I studied him closely. "There is something about you that makes you seem nice and affable, but there is something about your eyes that tells me that you're extremely shrewd. That you have experienced solving enough puzzles of your own, or maybe you're a little like me and you can't let something go."

His brow furrowed, and his gaze narrowed on me. "You're going to figure me out, aren't you?"

"Probably. Sorry. It's a hazard of the job. I tend to over analyze."

"That's okay. I'll just have to watch myself around you."

"Don't I remember you saying something about just coming back from somewhere?"

He sighed and shoved his hands in his pockets. "Yeah, the UK."

"Well, obviously the accent gives it away, so I can't claim to have guessed that."

He chuckled. "Yeah. I grew up splitting my time between the islands and London. My mother was a playwright. She's actually Welsh, come to think of it, but I was a London kid *and* a child of the islands."

"Oh, were your parents divorced?"

He shook his head. "Nope. I have one of those giant, super-tight-knit families. We just happen to be dispersed across the planet now. But no, it was just that every six months or so, I'd get popped into a different school so mum could have her West End run or whatever."

"Oh wow, that must have been a tough time but what an experience."

"Yeah, you could say that."

"So, you're here to what, be closer to your family?"

The furrow on his brow was imperceptible at first. It was fleeting. If I hadn't been watching him closely, I would have missed it. "Something like that."

"You're cagey. There's something I can't put my finger on with you."

His smile was sly. "I promise, what you see is what you get."

"Somehow I doubt that. Tell me something personal about you. So far all I know is you're great with Mayzie. Don't you find it weird practically living with someone and not knowing anything about them?"

He shrugged. "In my line of work, not really." He shoved his hands deeper into the pockets of his jeans, causing them to tug down and reveal a very brief strip of skin over his boxers I'd probably fantasize about all damn night. "Fair enough. I left for a girl. I had a plan that didn't quite work out the way I wanted. But I'm here now, so sometimes a blip in the plan leads you to exactly where you're supposed to be."

I smiled and nodded. "Sometimes you're supposed to look at something in a completely different way and then you feel—" I stopped talking and looked down at the journal.

Was I looking at this the wrong way? I closed it and steadied the spine in front of me as I'd been given it. Or at least I had *assumed* it was the front. I flipped it over to look at it the other way and realized I'd been looking at the damn thing backward and upside down. Damn it.

The layout of all the symbols still didn't read like a journal. It read more like a ledger. Like they were time stamps or date stamps, and possibly names. Locations, maybe? "Holy shit."

He stood straight. "What? Did I just solve it for you?"

I shook my head even as I grinned. "No, but you helped me see it better. Thank you."

"I don't even know what that means, but if it helped then I'm happy."

"Yeah, it's not a journal or a diary at all. It's a ledger. I think it was used to track, I don't know, I mean, it could be anything really. But you see how these are shortened symbols over here on the left, and the middle ones are slightly shorter, and then the ones at the right are two lines. I don't knowwhat the lines are. They could either be an address or an equation of some sort, but do you see what I mean?"

He leaned over. "Yeah, I see what you mean. But why would your friend leave you a ledger?"

"And *that* is the part of the puzzle I'm trying to get to. Why me?"

He grinned. "Well, when Ariel found out that you were a cryptanalyst, she got all geeked out and super excited. All I basically understood from anything she said was that you're a code cracker. Maybe Willa wanted you to be the one to crack the code."

JAX

Any second now, Neela was going to come down the stairs and my cover would be blown.

"Can we speed this along, please?" I tried to juggle the iPad as I put Mayzie in her highchair. I had my earphones in for this little team meeting, but I didn't want to have to answer any questions.

Ariel sighed. "Relax, Jax. Besides, she's getting ready for a meeting anyway. She's going to be a few minutes. It's fine."

"Yeah, it's fine for you. You're not the one on the undercover gig. You're living it up in bloody Hawaii."

"Now that you mention it, my tan is exemplary." She studied me closely. "Maybe it's time to rotate you out?"

But then I wouldn't see her every day. "I can bloody handle it."

"That's not what I'm saying. It's time to give you a break. You've been on all week. Let's rotate Trace in and give you a night off."

I was going to argue that I didn't need a night off, but that was a lie. I absolutely needed to get the hell away from here, or I was going to do something stupid. Extremely stupid. Something Ariel had strictly forbidden. Something I hadn't been able to stop thinking about since I saw her. So, maybe a night off wasn't the worst thing in the world. "Fine."

"Good. Now that that's settled, where are we on the journal?"

"She was working at it yesterday. She figured out that it's not really a journal but more of a ledger. She still doesn't have the language basis yet, but my money is that she'll get it soon. I know we've been spending some time looking at the ex, but I'm starting to think the kidnap attempt is related to Willa MacKenzie."

Trace pulled something up on the computer. "I found this the other day. It seems that the gallery sold several pieces to Ian Vanhorn. He's the head of Vanhorn Diamond Brokerage. They have their headquarters on Grand Cayman. He's also known in black market circles as Mr. Bad News. You don't go into a deal with him unless you are damn sure of yourself or just as dirty as he is. It's possible that people he worked with think that Neela has something of value."

Ariel frowned. "Okay, Vanhorn... what's his connection to Willa?"

Trace shook his head. "Other than the art he bought from her, I can't find one."

"Keep looking."

I frowned. *Ian Vanhorn?* "I feel like I've seen that name around the house somewhere."

Ariel turned her gaze on me. "In the house? A file? What?"

"Maybe in the office. I can't be sure until I go back in there."

Her gaze flickered up the stairs behind me. "Do you think you can get in her office and find out for sure?"

"Yeah. I'll figure it out."

Trace grinned at me. "Yeah, you will."

I ignored him. *Arsehole.*

He shrugged and leaned back in his chair then shot me a text.

Trace: *Don't worry. I won't tell. And I have to say you are being a very good boy because Neela Wellbrook is nice. She's absolutely smarter than you. Hell, she's smarter than everyone in here, except for Ariel. And God, that body. She's beautiful. So I don't blame you.*

Me: *Blame me for what?*

Trace: *Sporting that constant prepubescent boner.*

Me: *Are you always an asshole?*

Trace grinned as he tapped out his reply.

Trace: *I prefer to think of it as bullshit challenged.*

Me: *Whatever. It's not like that. My job is the kid.*

He chuckled low and sat back.

Trace: *Oh yeah, you tell yourself that your entire job is that kid and that you're not at all focusing any of your attention on hot mommy there. I believe you.*

I scowled at him and turned my attention back to Ariel. The problem was he was right. I *was* hot for her. From the moment she walked into a room, it was like my internal compass only turned toward her as true north. It was annoying. Not to mention, reckless.

Neela chose that moment to come down the stairs. "Morning." I tried for a neutral smile. "Sorry still on the call."

"It's no problem." She leaned down to the table to give Mayzie a kiss before grabbing a cup of coffee.

I didn't dare watch her openly. Instead, I watched her in my peripheral vision. She was freshly showered. Her hair was still damp and curling slightly on the ends. She wore a white and navy-blue shirt with black pinstriped pants. And she had the slightest hint of belly whenever she moved, looking so sexy I could lick her.

No. No licking.

I shook myself out of it. "Would you like some breakfast?"

A chime sounded on my phone, and I ignored it. I didn't need Trace's bullshit.

Double duty was bad enough. But the sooner we could find out who was after her, the better. Because I wasn't sure how much longer I was going to last.

Chapter Twelve

JAX

"Let's make this quick."

Trace grinned at me. "Easy, does it. Remember, I'm a hot manny too."

I rolled my eyes. "She's next door working, so if we can move this along before my cover is blown, that would be awesome."

He rolled his eyes. "Okay, okay. Where is the library?"

"This way."

Once we were in the library, I quickly checked my phone for the monitor on Mayzie's room She was down for a nap. Getting the kid on schedule hadn't been too bad. And thank fuck I knew how to do that. All those years with my nieces and nephews had taught me a thing or two. And Mayzie was a sweet kid. She gave Neela a run for her money, though.

That baby was willful, but she could be so, so sweet.

"Checking on the kid?"

I gave him a brief nod. "Neela is persnickety, so don't move anything you can't put back the way you found it."

He gave me a brief nod. "Not my first rodeo, but thanks for your *input*." His sarcasm dripped off of every word.

"Do you have to be a dick?"

"Yeah, well, when you have a big one."

"My experience is when someone talks about having a big dick, it's quite the opposite."

He gave me a chuckle. "Okay. So, Ian Vanhorn. Are you sure you saw something about him in here?"

I nodded. "This is where she was the last time. We could check the living room too, but it's going to be risky. She's just across the courtyard."

"Did you set the perimeter alarms in case Neela comes near the main house?"

"Of course. It's not my first rodeo either."

He chuckled. "Touché."

We searched the office, but there wasn't much to find. Neela had her own system, but most of the things in here were Willa's and sort of haphazard. The office was neat. There weren't any papers lying around, but there were books and knick-knacks and useless things everywhere. Where the hell had I seen that name?

It took us about fifteen minutes to search the office, but we came up with nothing. Trace shook his head. "Anything?"

I shook mine. "Maybe the living room? The kitchen is useless. There is not much storage there, but we can look."

"Yup. Why don't you take the living room? I'll head upstairs. I'll look in her room, and the baby's. I'll see if anything pops. Don't worry, I won't go through Neela's underthings."

"You're disgusting."

"I'm not a perv. I just want to get a rise out of you."

"Why?"

"I want to see what you're made of. I'm wondering why Ariel came to you first. What makes you so special?"

"Maybe Ariel has a thing for Brits?"

"Yeah, you can be a teacher's pet all you want. Our boss is hot. She's feisty though. Something tells me, you have a thing for your client instead."

"Nope. I know better."

Trace grinned at me. "Sure you do."

He was jogging up the stairs in a second.

If Neela did find him upstairs, at least we could make it seem like he was relieving me of my shift.

Another twenty minutes later and he was back down the stairs. "Nothing."

I was still on the books when I noticed the box. "Bingo!"

He came over. "What is that?"

It was an ornate decorative box. But *Vanhorn* was inscribed on the bottom, under the lock. When I opened it, we both gasped.

"Is that—" Trace asked.

I nodded. "Fuck, I think so."

"He gave her a diamond music box?"

"Well, the music box isn't diamond. It looks like brass. But yeah, that figurine sure looks like diamonds. It could be crystal, but, I mean, it's Vanhorn."

He whistled low. "Do you think they were boning?"

"Who knows? But with a gift like this, something tells me the answer is yes."

He slid me a gaze. "Do you think that Vanhorn is Mayzie's dad?"

I shrugged. "There's no way of knowing. Ariel already checked the birth records. Willa didn't name one. Mayzie's father is unknown."

Trace shook his head. "So apparently she didn't want the father in the picture at all."

"Exactly, which, I don't know if that's a good or bad thing."

I lifted the box gently and looked underneath.

I frowned. "Do you see that there?"

Trace squinted. "Looks like a number of some sort."

"Grab your phone. Take a picture."

He snapped it and we placed the box back the way we found it and then gently shut it again.

"I'll send it to Ariel and see if she can make anything of it."

"Yeah. Thanks."

"Good day. Not many people would have noticed a fucking knick-knack."

I shrugged. "Well, let's hope it's something."

"Maybe it is, maybe it's not. But at least we know there is a connection between the deceased mommy and Ian Vanhorn. Like a real connection. Not just that he bought art from her before."

I rubbed the back of my neck. "I've got a bad feeling about this."

"Yeah, that makes two of us. Good thing the two of them have us watching their backs."

"Yeah, but we need to figure out who the hell is after them, and fast."

NEELA

The man cooked, and he cleaned. What was there not to like? And he apparently had a magic skill and a way of making things that maybe you *like* to eat. And so far, I did not have that skill.

The thing was he was always around.

Every time I turned around, there he was, being next to damn-near perfect. It was exhausting being so tense all the time. A few days with him, and I was ready to lose it.

My reprieve was work though. It had been the smartest decision I ever made to move me, Adam, and Bex to the guest house.

"Look, just go over there. You know you want to."

Bex came up behind me. I nearly jumped.

"Don't you have somewhere to be?"

She grinned at me. "Yes. I wanted to tell you that we got a payment from the city. So, yay for checks. I'm gonna go down and deposit it at the bank. And then we have a possible new contract from them as well. Basic security stuff. They want to upgrade the governor's security system with something completely unhackable. After the last time, you know."

Oh yeah, the last time. The former governor's whole database had been hacked. Including personal photos. "Where's Adam?"

"Client site. Former employee apparently locked the laptop so good, they can't open it. None of their encryption keys are working, so he went on down there to see if he could fix it."

I nodded. "Okay. I guess maybe I'll go have lunch with Mayzie."

Bex grinned. "I think that's an excellent idea."

She practically skipped out. What was wrong with her? She had certainly not been this happy when I'd been dating Richard. Matter of fact she spent most of her time scowling at him.

Stop it. He's not a potential date. He's not someone you can be with. So just chill.

I shook my head to clear it. I needed serenity or something. I stepped out of the guest house, careful to lock up after myself.

Though we were on private grounds behind gated security, old habits die hard. We had sensitive information there. The extra layer of security didn't hurt.

The sun shone on the courtyard. The birds of paradise were in full bloom, with their orange, green, yellow, and pink accents on display, flooding the place with an explosion of color. I did love this house, the courtyard, everything. But the courtyard was my favorite part. Being out there smelled like hibiscus and warmth and home.

We'd placed benches all around the courtyard garden. There was a large grassy space for Mayzie to play on, and the benches had soft, cushioned padding on them. So we could sit or lie down and read out there. I hoped that someday I would be able to take the time to actually do that.

I opened the back door into the kitchen and was shocked by a sight I never thought I'd see.

Jax was gyrating backwards and forward, and he was singing quite well and doing an excellent Mick Jagger impression. "I can't get no no-no-no…" Then he jumped and turned to Mayzie, wiggling his ass back and forth at me as he crooned out, "Satisfaction…"

Mayzie clapped her hands together and said something along the lines of, "Sa sa," in response.

I leaned against the door jamb watching them for a moment. She was happy. Truly happy. She had no idea her mother was gone. I would make sure to talk to her about Willa. Tell her what it was like to grow up with her beautiful mother and how full of life Willa had been.

But at the moment, she was a baby, and she didn't need to know any of that. She just needed to know that she was loved and taken care of, and Jax was doing a damn good job of showing her that.

He jumped around as if to give Mayzie the bootie shake view and stopped abruptly. He cleared his throat. "Oh. I didn't hear you come in. I need to get a chime for that door."

I grinned in response. "Oh no, don't stop on my account. I was quite enjoying the show." Oh crap. What was wrong with my mouth around this guy? I never said stuff like that. That was Bex's arena.

"No, I think we're quite done here."

"Oh, come on. That's the best show I've seen in weeks."

"Only in weeks? This is the best arse gyration on two continents."

I shook my head. "You haven't lived until you've seen Bex twerk. It's a sight."

He chuckled. "I'll bet. Now that you've seen my secret shame, I need to see yours. That's how this works."

I laughed and shook my head. "Nope. Never going to happen."

He narrowed his electric-blue gaze on me and I felt trapped, held in time and space by his words, "Never say never."

Mayzie laughed as she banged her hands on the table in front of her. "Sa sa. Sa sa."

Jax squirmed. "She's making me sing the song over and over and over."

"Oh, please allow me to have a front row seat."

"You're both going to make me do this aren't you?"

I nodded as I hooted. He went back to the sink and started humming low. Mayzie clapped her hands and giggled. I couldn't help but follow suit. "Oh, yeah. Show us what you got."

Jax jumped and turned, using her bottle as his microphone as he proceeded to dance all around the kitchen, using the bar, the countertops, and anything within reach as props. He even paused at one point to juggle a few lemons. "I can't get nooooo…"

Sure enough, Mayzie laughed her little head off.

And I was completely and utterly charmed as he proceeded to do his entire routine.

I was in so much trouble.

Finally, he stopped, and even though Mayzie demanded more 'Sa Sa,' he shook his head and checked the time. "Sorry love." He picked her up out of her high chair, and then fetched her bottle from the fridge. He cuddled her close as he slid it in the bottle warmer. Then turned his attention to me. "You're home for lunch?"

I shrugged. "I wanted baby cuddles. I didn't expect to already love her so much."

He smiled at me and then handed Mayzie off. "Yeah, kids will do that to you."

God, she was so squishy and soft, I could just smoosh her. But she beat me to it and clapped her hands on my cheeks, squeezing. Laughing, she said, "Sa sa."

Jax nodded from behind her. "Yeah, you do Sa sa. I need to see this."

I rolled my eyes. "I can't do that as well as Jax can."

I met his gaze. A small smile lit his lips. "Oh, come on, I'm sure your arse wiggling backward and forward is still a sight to behold." His tone was low, intimate, making parts of me clench.

Mayzie was no help. "Sa sa."

With her in my arms, I did a much mellower version of the song, making sure to include her so at least she'd be part of it. She loved it and squealed with delight.

The whole time, Jax's eyes stayed glued to mine. "I told you... a sight to behold."

Was he... No, he couldn't be. But it felt like he was flirting with me. Which was just... that would never happen. Why not? I cleaned up nice. But Jax was in a whole different league.

Guys like him went out with women like Willa. Women like Willa were vivacious and commanded everyone's attention. All the attention. Throughout our lives together, I'd always felt invisible around her.

The way Jax looked at me, though... it was like he *saw* me. I could not get that lopsided, half-smug smile out of my head. I saw it every single time I closed my eyes. And it was messing with me.

"I—I should get lunch."

He smiled. "Already on a plate for you in the fridge."

My brows popped. "What?"

"Your lunch. It's in the fridge."

Shit. I was keeping him. "You don't have to take care of me."

"Yes, I do. Nannies take care of the whole family. Including mum. Get used to it. So, you can either eat in here if you want, or you can go outside. Sit in the garden?"

Oh God, he was heaven with muscles. I could get used to him taking care of me.

No. Don't you dare. He won't be here forever. And you're paying him to take care of you.

I cleared my throat. "I'll eat outside with Mayzie if that's okay."

He smiled. "Of course, it's okay. You go on and take her out. I'll bring lunch out."

Jesus. I was going to fall for this guy.

JAX

I wasn't going to tell Ariel this. But I was pretty much a natural at the whole manny thing. I could handle this. I'd take care of the kid and be back in the Guard in no time.

Are you going to take care her mum too?

Damn it. I'd managed to go a whole ten minutes without thinking about Neela. What was that shit yesterday with the 'Nannies look after the whole family' thing? Even to me, that sounded like I was offering orgasms on tap.

Weren't you?

Fuck. I wanted to.

The baby was much easier to deal with. Wanting Neela was a whole other kettle of fish. I was going to need patience and control for that one.

As I pushed the baby along in her stroller, Mayzie handed me a block. When I took it from her with a wide beaming smile, she clapped and then pointed to her mouth.

"You want me to put this in my mouth?"

She clapped her hands. I wasn't sure what that meant, but I shook my head. "No, not for mouth, for playing, love. Bang it like this." I demonstrated as I banged it on the handle of her stroller.

She frowned, and I gave her back the block. Immediately, she put it in her mouth.

"Love, you can't eat everything. That's how little people get sick." Which reminded me, we'd have to actually baby proof the house soon. It was only partially baby proofed with electrical outlets covered, but that left a lot that Mayzie could get into.

Look at you. Easy does it. She's not yours.

I hadn't said anything to Ariel, but that was the problem with this assignment. The kid was fucking cute. Not just cute… it was the way she wrapped her arms around me and held on tight like a little a baby koala. It was getting into heart-melting territory.

She's not yours.

I knew that. I *needed* to remember that.

Just like her new mama.

Neela wasn't mine. I was here to do a job. Watch her back. Protect them both. It should be an easy job. It didn't stop all the filthy, dirty thoughts I had about her last night, knowing she was sleeping one room away.

For the most part, I hid all the thoughts about wrapping my hands around those delicate ankles, pulling her down the bed, and screwing her until her head hit the headboard again. Wash, rinse, repeat.

Thoughts like that had to stop. I *knew* that I had to stop, or she would notice.

Not like you didn't flirt with her last night.

I didn't exactly mean to flirt. It was just the way things came out. It sounded like innuendo. I'd never been more relieved than when she went up to take a bath.

I knew what the hell I was doing here. I knew what I had to get done. I knew better than to trust a big butt and a smile as the boys from BBD had told me.

Not that Neela's ass was anywhere near big. But it was the sentiment. She was beautiful, smart. She needed me. I recognized the symptoms. I wasn't dumb. This was my pattern.

And you need to break it.

I'd woken up resolute, and I'd resolved to stay the fuck away from Neela that day as much as possible. Trace was on Neela duty, just watching the house, so I'd taken Mayzie, grabbed her diaper bag, and then headed down to Mother and Light Studios for her Mommy and Me class.

It had been on the original calendar before Willa died. It was something they did weekly, and Neela didn't want to stop. She, of course, had a client meeting, so she wouldn't be joining us until after.

That left me with a viper's nest of nannies and moms.

When I walked in, every set of eyes flickered over to me. I was used to women looking at me. It was the eyes. I recognized they were an unusual color of blue. It was also the height. At nearly six feet four inches, there weren't a bunch of places I could easily hide.

The receptionist grinned at me, glanced down at Mayzie, and furtively glanced at my left hand before she stuck out her chest. "Hi. I don't think we've seen you here before."

"Yeah, I'm the new manny for Mayzie MacKenzie."

"Oh, so you're not her dad?"

I sighed and shook my head. "No, I'm not." *You're trying too hard sweetheart.* And while normally I didn't mind obvious, lately I was drawn to subtle and unassuming. *Like Neela.*

I wanted to ruffle that still core until it screamed. I needed help.

"Oh, this is great. We love having fresh blood." She stood and made an announcement to all the women and babies waiting in the foyer. "Everyone, get ready, we're going to go into the yoga studio with the babies."

I frowned. "Yoga? No one said anything about yoga."

"Yes, yoga. That's today's activity. It was on the calendar. It rotates from month to month."

I had a distinct urge to flee. Oh, I'd done yoga before. Just usually with my ex. *Naked.* Somehow, I didn't think that was how this yoga session was going to go. Though, given the looks that some of the moms were giving me, it might end up that way.

"Oh, fabulous. Yoga." Mayzie was making spitting sounds, like she was trying to copy the motor of a car. Over and over again. God, this kid was happy. I didn't know why she was giving Neela such a hard time.

I glanced down at her. "Okay, you're going to take it easy on me kiddo. It's been a while since I've stretched."

A beautiful blonde approached. Every inch of her was perfect. There was nothing out of place from her red snakeskin bottoms to her matching red snakeskin sports bra, but she was clearly manufactured.

"Oh good, maybe we can spot each other." She smiled and indicated her baby on her mat.

I gave her a noncommittal, "Uh-huh."

She wasn't deterred though. "Hi, I'm Alana, and that's Madison over there. I just wanted to welcome you to the class. And I hope that we'll be seeing more of you."

"Yeah, sure. This was on Mayzie's calendar, so I'm doing the activity."

"From what I remember, Mayzie's mom Willa wasn't exactly hands on. She usually brought a nanny along to do the yoga with Mayzie while she took one of the Bikram classes."

I lifted a brow, not missing a single dart of judgment. I refused to give this woman any indication of anything.

Still not deterred, she continued. "Well, we um, have a little social gathering afterward if you would like to join us. It's usually held at my house. You know, just a few moms and nannies, of course. So, you're welcome to come."

Yeah, I'd just bet I was. Was that where the naked yoga would happen?

Dick: *I like naked, but not this one. I get the impression she'll try and bronze me in the morning.*

"We'll see what little Mayzie here feels like."

Right on cue, Mayzie turned and booty-scooted in the exact opposite direction from Alana and Madison. God, I loved this baby more and more with her subtle judgments. What was it that my niece was always saying? Oh yes, *savage*.

I was surprised. The class was actually not bad. I couldn't

touch my toes for shit, but Mayzie seemed to have fun. It probably wasn't as relaxing for me as it could have been since I was on full watch-dog routine, but it wasn't too bad. Lots of fit mums in yoga pants. Not a bad view. But it was tricky keeping an eye on the exits.

Alana made herself a nuisance every chance she got though.

At one point when I was holding Mayzie up and doing basic leg lifts, she chose to try and help me 'correct my form.' I coughed when her hand traced over my upper thigh as if to indicate where I should be feeling the burn.

Dick: *Help me. I need an adult.*

It was on the tip of my tongue to let her know I'd been trained in four martial arts and was, for all intents and purposes, a lethal weapon when Neela barged in. She was harried, her dark hair still hanging thick and loose. But she'd changed into the tightest little pair of arse-hugging black leggings and a top that equal parts served up her tits to me and strapped them down. She looked ready to work out... or to fuck, if porn could be believed.

Dick: *This one please. You think she'll let me rub against her yoga pants?*

Jesus. Down mate. I was not going to think about all the practical, dirty reasons for downward dog. Professional, damn it. I could do this. Not think about her. Easy...

Was it me, or did her eyes narrow at Alana when she walked up? Her gaze when she turned to me was shuttered. But to Mayzie, she was all smiles. "Hi, baby girl."

Mayzie cooed and reached for her. I surrendered her easily. "If you want, I'll head outside." Yes, please God. I was going to pitch a bloody tent if I stayed in her proximity too long.

She blinked at me in surprise. "No. Why would you wait outside? You started you might as well finish. And class is meant for two parents, I think."

Alana's brow furrowed as she glared at Neela. "I'm sorry, do I know you?"

Neela's brows popped. "Alana, we were in school together from elementary through high school. You know me."

Alana batted her big dark eyes. "Oh, right. Neela something, right?"

"Yeah, it's Neela." She rolled her eyes and settled down next to Mayzie, who handed her the block. Neela played with it and tossed it back and forth with her hands, completely ignoring Alana.

Alana, however, was not to be deterred. She just sauntered back to her position, all the while glancing at me over her shoulder.

I don't know what made me do it. (**Dick**: *It was me. I made you do it.*) But I reached an arm around Neela, then rubbed her lower back. "Glad you made it."

It was an intimate move. Anyone watching would assume I was well accustomed to touching her. And Christ, would I love for them to be right

She stiffened slightly at first but then melted into my touch. She smelled of honey and lime. "Thank you for bringing Mayzie." Her voice was soft and smooth and intimate.

Alana looked back and forth between Mayzie and me, and then Neela, and then back again. She opened her mouth but then snapped it shut.

Then Neela reached up on tiptoe and planted a kiss on my cheek. One I could feel all the way to my bones.

Oh shite. All systems revved to full alert. *Ease up lads. It was a simple kiss. Let's not get all excited.*

Dick: *Nope. All systems go.*

My muscles went rigid, and all of the blood in my body

123

rushed south. Cock, basically ready for action. Luckily, Neela was distracted by evil mum.

Alana frowned. "Uh, I don't remember you with a baby."

"Well, I'm Mayzie's guardian. So, if you'll excuse us, we don't want to hold up class."

And then Neela placed the mat she'd brought next to mine and sat down. Mayzie scooted on over to Neela's mat and proceeded to roll onto her back and try to eat her toes.

We all resolutely ignored Alana, who couldn't have been more pissed off. Well, it served her right.

I leaned over and whispered, "That happen a lot?"

"Sorry. She was part of the bitch brigade in high school. I couldn't resist."

I leaned back over, making sure my lips were close to her ear. "Feel free to use me as a prop any time."

I'd gotten rid of Alana, but now I had a whole new problem. Neela. I couldn't take my fucking eyes off of her.

Unlike most of the women in this room, she didn't look like she was trying too hard. Her leggings were simple. Black. There was some mesh and something that was on the side, and she was baring her midriff too. Clearly, the woman worked out.

I didn't know when she had time, but wow. Flat, tight. Perky tits. And I just wanted to bury my face between them. Next to me on the mat, Mayzie continued to bang her block and proceeded to make the revving-motor sound again.

I smiled down at her. "Right, love. I'd love to motorboat too," I muttered quietly.

I probably shouldn't say more of those words to the baby.

"By the way, thank you for doing this for me. I'm pretty sure this is above and beyond the call of duty."

I shrugged. "That's all right. That's kind of how this goes. You didn't even have to come."

Dick: *I'll show her a hundred and one ways to come.*

I squeezed my eyes shut. I was devolving into a caveman.

She frowned. " I promised I'd keep her commitments. I don't want to change anything on her. And well, we need to bond."

"See, I told you. Already a great mum."

SEBASTIAN

Penny sat cross-legged on our bed, staring at the bay with those big, dark eyes. She was wearing overalls, and there was green paint on the end of one of her curls. I couldn't help but grin at her. "You know, you're beautiful."

She scrunched up her nose and shook her head. "You're still not answering my question. Where are you going?"

"I'm going to go see Tristan. I just want to check in on him, make sure he's okay. We spoke on the phone, but he's somehow convinced that what happened was an isolated incident and it had nothing to do with him and more to do with the event, which I don't buy."

Now there was a frown creasing her forehead. I reached out and rubbed my thumbs over the slight crease. "Don't frown."

She smacked my hands away. "I will frown if I want to. Are you sure it's wise to go see him?"

"Jesus, I'll have a guard with me."

"Correction, you'll have ten. My father already told me. But, can we trust them all?"

"I have to trust them. And you know full well I can take care of myself."

She pressed her lips together into a tight line. I knew that look. She wasn't pleased. "Well, if you won't let me travel alone with the Guard, then why should I let you travel alone with the Guard?"

I sighed. "Look, the guards are loyal to me."

"Yeah, well some of them were loyal to *them*."

I winced. She was right. After the conspiracy of the last three years to unseat me, we were all on edge, though everything had turned out okay in the end.

I had my brother and my sister. We were all together. We'd prevailed. But still… we'd taken some losses. My father for one. Jessa's adopted father. They'd nearly killed Penny more than once. Nearly killed me. They certainly tried to kill Lucas, but my brother proved craftier than anyone ever anticipated. I hoped things were settling down and we'd weeded out any and all conspirators.

But the fact that my cousin was in danger led me to believe that everything was not smooth sailing, so I needed to see him. I also wanted to talk to my uncle. Despite what had happened, I knew he didn't have any part in any of the treasonous plots.

I needed to speak to him about my plan, or rather Penny's plan, to bring back the knights. Because if that was something I could do without the approval of the Council, then I could provide Tristan with protection and give myself a team of people I trusted who couldn't be swayed by the Council. "I'll only be gone two nights, okay?"

"Then why can't I come with you?"

"Well, for starters, you might be pregnant. So, I'd rather we not travel together. If you're carrying an heir and something happens to us, that means Lucas is in charge. Do you really think that's a good idea?"

She raised her brow, and then she snorted. "You know that's ridiculous. I can pee on a stick right now and tell you I'm not pregnant. But you make a really good point. No one wants Lucas to be in charge."

I laughed. My brother was completely capable. And, knock on wood, if something did happen to us, he would run the country how he thought I'd want it to be run. But Lucas had a tendency to get himself into trouble, and Jessa was still finding her feet, so there was no need to give them any unnecessary headache. "You stay here. It's two nights."

She pouted, rolling her eyes. "Fine."

I cursed under my breath. " I do need you to do me a favor. Can you go see Ariel?"

She sat up with a grin. "There is no need to ask me to go see my bestie. I was bummed that you canceled game night the other night."

I nodded. "Sorry about that. After the Council meeting, I was in a bit of a mood."

She was still grinning when she said, "I think I improved your mood considerably."

"Why, yes, you did." I studied her dark eyes. "I don't want you to think that you can't see Ariel."

"I know that. It's just that things have been really busy. There was the new benefit event to plan, and I just haven't had the chance during the week to see her. And it was so much more convenient before she left. She was right down the hall."

"I know. For what it's worth, I did try to convince her that we should fight to keep her."

She shook her head. "I know. I also know Ariel. She wouldn't have wanted you to throw your weight around on her behalf."

The wash of shame was hard to swallow. I felt like I hadn't done enough. But maybe, if Uncle Roland gave me the information that I needed, I'd be able to do right by her.

"Ariel would have left on her own anyway. She knows the rules. She knows the laws. And she might sometimes seem like she bends the rules to fit whatever purpose she needs, but at the end of the day, Ariel is a loyalist. She would do anything for the Winston Isles."

"But this was her home, and she is your family. I never wanted her to feel like she had to leave. And as king, it seemed ridiculous that she wouldn't let me do anything to stop it from happening."

Penny rose up on her knees and crawled over to me, sliding her hands up over my shirt and looping them around my neck. "I know you wanted to do more. You wanted to save my best friend, but my best friend doesn't *need* saving. She's Ariel. She'll tell you *she* does the saving."

I chuckled low, wrapped my arms around Penny's waist, and pulled her close. "I know. I just hate that you don't get to see her as often. And she probably feels alone and isolated herself."

"Look, I'm mostly done with the benefit stuff. I'll go see her. I mean, I know you're going to insist on a massive entourage, or will you let me go clandestine-like?"

I scowled at her. Penny was notorious for slipping her guard. My stomach still turned when I thought about the number of times she'd gone to see Robert, the traitor, trying to get him to confess to the conspiracy. She'd done that without a guard, without supervision, without anyone to watch her back.

Ariel was watching her back.

Yes, she was. But I hadn't known that, and anything could have happened. As it was, Robert Sandstorm died in her arms because a member of his bloody conspiracy thought he might talk. Penny had come far too close to dying that day. As far as I was concerned, anywhere she went that was not in this palace required a forty-man team. "Fine, tell your father. He'll provide the appropriate guard."

She quickly unhooked her arms, but I refused to let her go.

"Sebastian, I'm not a child."

"No, you are not. But you might be carrying *my* child, so you need full protection."

She shook her head. "No. You try and do that, and I will slip my guard."

I tightened my grip on her hips. "You will not."

"You can't force me. You won't be here."

"Woman, I swear to God, I will handcuff you to this bed and have the staff bring in food. And they will hand feed it to you because you won't have the use of your arms or your legs."

She shimmied. "Ooh, sexy. But no, you will not cuff me to the bed. You will not give me a full guard. I'll take five. And it's ridiculous for me to take that many because they'll basically announce my arrival anywhere on the island. You've gone overboard with the protection. You forget I *am* a guard."

"Were."

"Present. *Am.* I'm still on the Intelligence team. You and I, we had a deal. If I don't take unnecessary risks, you relax on the whole hyper-protection thing. I'm not taking forty people with me to go see my bestie to drink wine and insult my husband."

I lifted a brow. "Your husband is perfect. There is nothing to insult."

She smacked me on the shoulder. "Oh, so much to insult."

I gave her a sly grin and leaned in to nuzzle my nose to hers. "I'm just trying to protect you. What if you're pregnant?"

"Listen dumbass, women have been pregnant for centuries. But I doubt I am."

"Hey, you stopped taking the pill. You were ovulating the last time. You *could* be pregnant."

"Oh my God, why do you know my ovulation schedule? You are insane about this."

Maybe I was a little insane.

I knew it was my job to produce an heir. Not that I didn't already want a child with Penny, a little version of me and her with dark curls running down the halls. But I wanted to carry on my father's legacy, and my child would need protection. "All agreements we made before are null and void. If you're pregnant, you become a huge target."

"No. Our agreement stands, or I'll make your life extremely difficult. If I'm not pregnant, you're cut off." She shoved against my shoulders. I didn't budge. She narrowed her gaze, and I saw the murder in her eyes. Then I voluntarily let her go and stepped back.

I was a little afraid of her. She might not be able to entirely beat my ass, but she could make my life difficult. She was a hell of a fighter. "Okay, okay. Not null and void. I just—" How did I make her understand? "I want you to be careful."

"Like I said, I will take five guards. And you forget, I'm going to see my bestie. She was one of the best Royal Guards you've ever had. So, relax."

I cracked my neck. "Fine."

She grinned. "Was that so hard?"

"Yes. Yes, it was."

"You go see your cousin and your uncle. Then create your own Knights of the Round Table."

I rolled my eyes. "Why do I get the impression you're getting a huge kick out of this?"

She practically danced up on her knees, making the bed bounce as she did so.

"I married a King Arthur."

I rolled my eyes. "Sebastian. My name is Sebastian."

She waved her hand. "Uh, same difference. I'm Guinevere, minus the whole sleeping-with-Lancelot thing."

I scowled at her. "You're not sleeping with Roone."

She wrinkled her nose. "He is pretty. *Really* pretty. I mean, have you seen those muscles?"

I prowled toward her, my frown deepening. "What?"

She giggled as she backed up. "I mean, he *is* pretty. But I don't like to be told what to do. He has that whole me-caveman-you-follow thing going for him. Not my cup of tea."

"I can be a caveman."

She grinned. "Oh, you could try. But I have your number."

I reached the edge of the bed and stared down at her. She did have my number. In the end, I would give her whatever she wanted because she had my heart. "You think you have my number?"

"Oh, I know I do."

"Well in that case, maybe it's time for me to show you who's boss?"

She giggled. "I thought you had to pack."

"I have people for that. Besides, if I'm going to have Knights of the Round Table, I need to remind my wife who gives her all the good orgasms."

She giggled and scooted back. Then she leaped off the bed, running and squealing through our quarters as she went. I couldn't help my laugh as I took off after her.

Chapter Thirteen

NEELA

Motherhood was a trip.

For the first time in my career, I'd ended a meeting early. Or in the case of Zap World Technologies, on time. Whenever we had a team meeting, they always dragged it out and then would slide in additional scope requests at the very end. So this time when they walked in, I was very clear with them. "This meeting starts on time and ends on time. Anyone who comes late, well, they're shit out of luck."

The vice president couldn't believe it when he walked in fifteen minutes late and I didn't stop the meeting to introduce him. And every time he'd try to ask a question, I cut him off and let him know that we'd already covered it at the beginning and he could discuss it with one of his colleagues at the end.

Before, I never would have spoken to a client like that. But I was going to set boundaries. I had to. Otherwise, I was never going to survive. Oddly enough, the VP wanted to add contracts for two more projects.

They were a gaming company and wanted us to help them build an unhackable game. Their last game had performed so well they had an influx of cash.

I told him to set up another meeting, and then I left.

It felt amazing. Boundaries were my friends.

Also, watching Jax Reynolds do downward dog and seeing just how flexible that man was? #worthit

And Mayzie was warming to me now. She wanted me to carry her out of the Mommy and Me class instead of Jax. And as we walked, she happily gurgled and placed her little fat hands to my mouth and mimicked kissing sounds. "You want a kiss?"

All she said in response was a gurgle, but I placed a little kiss on her chubby cheek and she clung to me tighter. My heart broke just a little. This poor little girl. She would never know her mother. But that was okay. I would make sure to remind her with a little bit of Willa every day, so she would always remember her.

Jax pointed out his car. "I've texted Trace. He's supposed to relieve me when we get back. We'll take my car back."

"You know, I was actually thinking maybe lunch out would be okay?"

He frowned. "Oh, I didn't see that on the schedule for the day."

"I know, I just... Mayzie's finally beginning to like me, so I don't want it to end just yet."

He sighed and nodded, pulling out his phone and sending a text to someone.

"You letting Trace know?"

He nodded.

"I'm sorry. You should go. I can handle one little baby

through lunch."

Jax gave me one of his lopsided smiles. "I already told you, what you need, I'll provide. The shift change can wait."

How bad was it that I was thinking about all of my other needs? And just how well he could provide for them.

He opened the door to the restaurant for us. As we walked in though, right in the waiting area, I saw the one person I didn't want to see.

Richard. Dick.

He stood, his gaze landing on me with the baby in my arms. "Neela? What are you doing here?"

Jax was quick. He immediately placed himself between me and Dick.

Richard scowled. "Who the fuck is this?"

Did he mean Jax or Mayzie? "None of your business."

Richard's skin flushed, and he muttered under his breath. "Actually, it might be. If you have some new boyfriend and are playing happy family, I get to know about it for the next few weeks."

Jax scowled down at Richard. "Neela, who is this guy?"

"The ex."

Richard tried to step around Jax, but Jax blocked his path. "Right. Well, I'm the guy who doesn't like you getting quite so close to Neela and the baby. So, I'm going to need you to back it up."

Richard frowned but did as he was told, and I breathed a sigh of relief.

I stepped back around Jax. "It's fine. Richard can't hurt me anymore, he's just an old acquaintance."

Richard's brows shot up. "Acquaintance? We were going to get married."

I frowned. "In what world? Was that before or after you

stole my company from me?"

"Well, that was where I always meant for it to go."

"I didn't know imaginary engagement rings were a thing."

Jax chuckled and took Mayzie from me. She went to him easily, and he nuzzled her. "Let me put our name in for a table. You okay?"

"Yep. I can handle this."

As Jax went up to the hostess and presumably gave our names, Dick couldn't take his eyes off him. "Who is that asshole?"

"That asshole is none of your business." This was fun. Giving as good as it got, refusing to back down, I was digging it.

"Look, we didn't even break up that long ago. Were you seeing him while you were dating me? That would explain why you never had time for me."

I sighed. "Richard, not everything is about you."

It seemed that Jax had every intention of being my savior all day, because he put a hand on my lower back and leaned close, whispering. "Our table will be ready in a minute. I'm just doing this to irritate him."

I couldn't help myself. I giggled.

I turned to meet Jax's gaze, and that intense, icy-blue stare was on me. Unwavering. So intense I dared not look away.

"Excuse me, do you mind? I'm trying to talk to my girlfriend," Richard tried to interrupt.

Jax didn't take his eyes off me. Instead, he said, "Ex."

"Well, if you would give us a moment, I'd like to change that."

I gawped at him. "What?"

Just at that moment, the buzzer we'd been given rang. Our table was ready. "See you around," I muttered.

Richard marched after us. "No, wait. Listen, can I come by

the office?"

"I'm busy."

"I know. But you know, maybe we should talk."

"Well, like I said, I'm very busy. Why don't you call Bex and make an appointment?"

Then I followed behind Jax, his broad shoulders parting the sea of people for me.

Chapter fourteen

ARIEL

Hawaii was a long way away, but at least Tamsin was coming on board. She'd arrive tomorrow. I had one team member left to gather. Zia. God help me, the clients had better be there.

I knew right away something was off. The hairs on the back of my neck stood at attention. I parked in my spot right out front and couldn't shake the feeling something was amiss. A quick scan of my surroundings told me what the problem was. There were a half-dozen Royal Guard in civilian clothes milling about on my block.

So the question was, who was in my office, Sebastian, Penny, Jessa or Lucas? Bryna didn't get a guard yet as she and Lucas were merely engaged.

I knew as soon as I walked in.

"Were you even going to tell me that you were in Hawaii?"

I'd been dodging her calls a little lately. I didn't want to hear pity and concern in Penny's voice.

"Hey Pen. Who let you in?"

She grinned. "A very good-looking blond gentleman. Nice and tall with what I imagine are an excellent set of abs under his shirt."

I snorted a laugh. "Oh my God. Of course, he would just let you in. What did you say?"

"Well, I said that you were my bestie and that I was the queen, and he had to let me in by royal decree."

I rolled my eyes. "What did you really say?"

"I said I had an appointment with you and asked if I could wait inside."

I called out. "Trace, you're fired."

From somewhere in the kitchen, he chuckled. "You think I don't recognize the Queen of the Winston Isles? She could have told me anything and I'd still have let her in."

"She could have been here to rob us."

"Well technically, this is her island, so she can do what she wants."

Penny nodded. "Yup. I own the whole place. Actually, my husband does. But I own all the paint."

I laughed. Penny was a sometimes artist. Well, an all-the-time artist, really. She just had more responsibilities since becoming queen and didn't get to paint as much. "God, I miss you."

She bounded over and gave me a big hug. I noticed that she'd already taken off her shoes and made herself quite comfortable.

"Do I even need to ask?"

"No. Sebastian told me you were coming back tonight. I'd called you several times, you hadn't responded. I had to learn about your trip from my husband. Imagine the way he gloated."

I rolled my eyes. "Asshole."

She nodded. "I completely agree. Besides, I needed to escape the palace. The man can't keep his hands off me."

"Oh, woe is you."

"I'm telling you. My vagina hurts."

From the kitchen Trace coughed. "Ew. I think I'm just gonna go to the study."

I laughed and then led Penny through the dining area and into my back office. "Have a seat."

Penny laughed. "As if you had to tell me twice." She carried her Louboutins in one hand and her backpack over her shoulder.

I shook my head. "Same old Penny. Whose bright idea were the shoes?"

"Well, I had to make Sebastian think that I had a very important meeting. Otherwise, he would have insisted on one more shag before I left. And like I said, my vagina hurts. I mean I love the attention, don't get me wrong. But seriously, I tell the man yes let's have a baby, all he wants to do is try. I'm not even ovulating."

I laughed. "How is this different from any other time?"

"Well, now it's like he's on a serious let's-make-a-baby train, and if we're not actually making a baby, we're practicing. Several times a day practicing. I'm tired. I need sleep. Can I sleep here?" She pleaded with me.

"Sure, but you know he'll know where to find you, right?"

"Ugh, I need other friends."

"He knows all your friends. You'll either be here or at Bryna and Jinx's. Where else you gonna go?"

"My parents. I can go to my parents' house."

"You realize your dad works for him, right? Your dad would give you up."

"Not if I told him my vajayjay hurts."

I spat out the sip of water I was taking. "Oh my God, if you tell Ethan that I will pay you money. All the money I have in my purse right now."

She rolled her eyes. "I know you don't carry cash. That's a sucker's bet."

I giggled. "Fair enough. You caught me. To what do I owe the lovely visit? I would have seen you later today anyway."

She cocked her head. "Why?"

I lifted a brow. "Your husband didn't tell you? He summoned me to the palace. He said there was some problem he wants me to look at."

She shook her head. "I have no idea what that's about. But I will find out. He's gone for a couple of days anyway, so I guess your meeting has been postponed."

"I don't know. I just—" I paused. What was I trying to say? "I feel like this will be my first official visit. I'm a little nervous."

"Why? You know the palace is your home."

"I know, I know, I just… I mean my past, you know?"

She nodded. "I'm so sorry. I wish there was more I could have done."

"No. Look, Sebastian has needed to go to battle with the council twice now. For his brother and sister. And there will be other times when he needs to go to battle. I don't want to be one of the reasons. Okay?"

She shrugged. "I guess, but it still sucks."

"You'll see me all the time anyway."

"Yes, I know. So why are you avoiding my calls?"

I shook my head. "I'm not avoiding your calls. I'm on recruiting missions. I've got three team members signed, and I have another two recruitments to do. The last two are local though."

She sat up and grinned. "Zia?"

I laughed. "Yes, Zia."

Zia Montgomery had trained with us in the Guard. There'd been this one guard, a total prick. We didn't think he'd make it to final selection, but he kept moving up because he was so good at fooling everyone. One night we'd all been out at a bar, and he'd hit on Zia pretty aggressively and wouldn't let up. Finally, he put his hands on her ass and basically forced her onto his lap. Well, Zia hadn't taken much of a liking to that, and the guy had ended up with two black eyes, a broken nose, and missing two teeth. Zia was about five foot two and a complete firecracker. We loved her immensely.

Unfortunately, she'd been booted from training for 'conduct unbecoming.' We had howled and fought and begged Ethan, Penny's father, to let her stay.

But he couldn't make an exception. Violence against another member of the Royal Guard was strictly forbidden. Luckily, the asshole had been booted as well, because the moment Zia had handed him his ass on a platter, several other women had come forward too. He'd been a nuisance. And everyone had been afraid to speak up. So Zia had never been Royal Guard, but she joined the Royal Police Force instead. Which was great because I needed someone who was basically a badass and wasn't afraid to fight for what she wanted. I just hoped I could pay more than the police force.

Penny said, "I can't wait to see her. It's been a while. You know, we used to regularly do lunch and stuff. But then she moved to the other island, and I haven't seen her much."

"Yeah, that's the part that sucks. Like the ferries are super convenient, but no one really thinks to take them very often."

"Yeah. It's like having a friend who lives in Brooklyn. You know it's super close, but you just don't see them as much unless you're going out in Brooklyn to party."

I shrugged. "Yeah I guess."

"I forget you didn't really spend a lot of time playing around in New York."

"Nope, I was too busy watching your ass."

"Yeah, well. I was too busy watching Sebastian's ass."

I grinned. "Literally and figuratively."

"Yeah, yeah, I shagged the prince. That was not my intention when I went to New York. You know that."

"Yes, I know. You were very valiant in your effort to hold off. It took you what, a whole month before you shagged him?"

"I might add that it was your idea to get super-duper close to him."

"I said get close to the man. I didn't say shag him."

"Ugh, I know." Penny wisely shifted the focus to me. "So, what's your deal? Did you decide to try that dating app we talked about?"

I groaned. "No, I told you I do not have time to date. I need to build a business. Get my life off the ground."

"God and Jesus Christ, I just wish you would let me meddle in your life like you meddle in mine."

I grinned. "Nope, no can do."

"Babe, have you ever even been in love? It's awesome."

I don't know what it was, the way she said it or the grin and the light in her eyes that made me realize I'd never even told her that I'd been in love once. I'd never even told her that I'd had my heart broken or who'd broken it. Who doesn't tell their best friend that?

It was one of those things that was like the secret white elephant in the room that I'd managed to camouflage so she wouldn't see it. But I'd been desperate to talk it about ever since I'd seen that stupid Google alert.

"Once."

She sat up off my settee and frowned at me. "With who?

And I know you don't mean Michael."

I'd had a very-much-unrequited crush on her brother. And honestly, looking back, Michael had been more of a habit. A replacement for the person I really wanted. I figured if I could just always have a go-to guy to crush on, no one would ever ask too many questions or look too closely as to why I never let anyone get close. And while I'd had a crush on Michael, I it wasn't really in that way of a person that you are so obsessed over that you can't function, you can't think, and all you want to do is be with them. No. Because I'd been in love with someone else.

"I—" What the hell did I say?

How about the truth?

"Prince Tristan."

Her eyes went wide. "Prince Tristan? You were in love with him?"

I sighed. "Remember that summer your parents sent you on that training trip? You were in Miami from the end of the school term up until August."

"Yeah. I remember. But we talked basically every day."

"I know. I just kind of *omitted* him."

Her mouth unhinged. "No. I would have known if you were in love, I mean—" She stopped herself. And I could almost see the gears in her brain working as she tried to put the pieces together. "We talked every day, and I remember you got a job, and—" Her gaze flickered to mine, and she stared at me. "Oh my God. You totally omitted *everything*."

I flushed. "Yeah."

"We are gonna talk about that later. You've been hiding something from me for years." She scowled. "Oh my God, like ten years."

"I know." I should never have said anything. She would never let this go. That was Penny for you. Once she had her teeth in something, forget it.

"We'll discuss. But first, spill."

I groaned. "It wasn't even… I don't know. You weren't there, and he came into the movie theater where I worked. Remember that place?"

She nodded. "Yeah, McGill's. Like the old-timey place. It had proper old-school fountain machines and cotton candy and popcorn. The floors were super sticky. It played all the latest movies, but it had a vintage feel."

"Yeah, McGill's. I loved that place. He did too. He'd come in for matinees. And one day he just, I don't know, asked me to join him. It was raining. No one was in there, and I was supposed to be working the projector anyway. So I turned the movie on and joined him. And we just, I don't know, talked I guess. Connected. I don't even remember what was showing, some action movie. And we hit it off. He came back the next day. And he kept coming back for two weeks straight. I remember he was often at boarding school. I didn't know why he didn't spend his time doing fun island-prince things." I shrugged. "Maybe he was trying to avoid his brother."

"Or maybe he really liked you." Penny sat forward. "Oh my God, I need popcorn."

"You do not need popcorn. It's not that much of a… It's nothing."

"It doesn't sound like nothing. How did I not know about Prince Tristan? Jesus. Never mind, continue."

"You're so dramatic."

"I'm sorry, but if I'd had a secret love affair with Sebastian and kept it from you… You would need to know all the details."

"Oh my God, you *did* have a secret love affair with Sebastian, and—"

Wait a minute. She *hadn't* told me, and I'd been furious

when I found out.

"You know to be fair, I found out on my own. But yes, I was also irritated."

"See."

"Fair enough, you have a point. You can yell at me later. But yeah, we started seeing each other. All the time. Every day. And you know how things were at home for me. I basically never wanted to be there. And well, he was in the palace, so I couldn't exactly just waltz up there. Especially when you weren't there. So we were at the theater a lot and on the beach the rest of the time. You know, those caves down on Prince's Beach."

"Yeah, but Prince's Beach is closed to the public after six p.m."

"Yes, but remember, *he's* not the public."

She grinned. "Oh my God, you guys had a secret love den."

"Yeah, I guess. It was our spot. There was a cabana down there that was basically never used, and we would just hang out there."

She sat up and grinned. "Oh my God, by hang out do you mean—"

I shook my head. "No. You know I lost my virginity to Tommy Wall our freshman year of uni."

She rolled her eyes. "God, I wish he hadn't been your first. He was a dud."

"Yeah, he was a dud. But at that point, I figured I'd better just get rid of the damn thing."

"I wish you hadn't done that."

"Yeah, me too, but I was just like 'let's get this party over with.'"

She laughed. "Yeah, that totally sounds like you too."

"So anyway, we would watch the stars and just spend all this time together. And you know he was playing soccer *all* the time, so he would have these matches and I would watch them on the telly. Then whenever he would come back, I'd be the first person he would see. He'd text me and say, 'Meet me at our place.' And we were, you know, just two dumb kids in love."

I sighed. "He had this whole plan for what we were going to do. He was going to go to school in the UK while he also trained with one of the teams there. And I was going to take my credits and transfer to a school over there. We'd worked it all out. I'd done all the paperwork. We were supposed to go on a trip over there together before the end of the summer. You know my dad barely even noticed when I wasn't there, and you were already in the States. So I got time off work, and we were gonna go for a week. See how I liked it, make sure I wanted to go through with it, and the whole thing. We bought the tickets, and we were ready to go."

She nodded, encouraging me to continue. "What happened?"

"Well, my last day at work, I waited for him to pick me up so that we could go. I knew exactly which flight it was. I knew everything. I was bags-packed and ready to move. But he never showed up."

She blinked at me. "What?"

"Yeah. That was it. I never saw him again."

She frowned and shook her head. "Wait, no. Okay so the summer we were sixteen, he was I think, what, eighteen?"

I nodded. "I know what you're doing. You're trying to time what happened. Basically, he left me to go play for Real Madrid."

"But—he—He could have taken you with him. It would have been—"

"Yeah, I know. It would have been a different airline ticket. No big deal. Madrid instead of London. But that was it."

"Do you think his parents found out and stopped him?"

"I don't know. The point is he never called, he never wrote, nothing. No text, no Facebook message, no nothing. Just done. Worst part was, it was Ashton who told me. I thought maybe I'd messed up our meeting spot or time, but when I went to the beach to look for him, his brother was there."

She shuddered. "My God. I'm going to kill him. I know where he is. I will just go and kill him. That's it."

I eyed her. I was ordinarily the one more prone to violence, but Penny could surprise you. She looked all sweetness and light, but she had a streak in her. She was very protective. "No, he's not worth it. It was nearly a decade ago. It doesn't matter now."

"What do you mean it doesn't matter now? He left you. You guys had plans."

"You see why I don't talk about it. It makes me angry. It makes me feel dumb. It makes me feel used. I mean, God, I would have given him anything. A part of me doesn't even understand how it happened between us. He didn't even get anything out of the deal. It's not like I slept with him."

Then hopeful Penny made an appearance. "But what if something stopped him? What if he was trying to come and get you, and you know his brother, Ashton the fucktard, what if he found out and was gonna tell his parents? Or—"

I shook my head. "No. Don't make excuses for him. He knew my number and he didn't contact me. He just didn't want me. Or maybe he got bored or decided there was someone else he'd rather be with."

"God, I am so sorry that I never knew."

"I know. And I'm sorry I never told you. I was embarrassed and just felt, I don't know, dumb. And sad."

She frowned. "But, I came back, and you never said a word."

"I know. I didn't want you feeling sorry for me. And I also didn't want you hopping on a plane to go kick his ass."

"I totally would have done that."

"I know."

"I remember you being down in the dumps or something. I couldn't quite place it, but you were not yourself."

"I tried to cover it and ask you about your trip and how it was and stuff, but it hurt."

She nodded. "And right after that was when you kind of doubled down on your Michael crush."

"Yeah. It gave me a distraction, something else to think about."

"Jesus Christ, Ariel. You haven't seen him at all since then?"

"No. I mean, he hasn't been home much. And any time he was home, I would ask Ethan for other assignments."

"Oh my God. You have been avoiding him for ten years."

"Yeah. Healthy, right?"

"No. Not healthy at all."

I shrugged. "Yeah, well. You do what you have to do to survive."

"And how do you feel now?"

"Fine I guess. I don't think about him much."

She lifted a brow. I hated that she could discern when I was lying so quickly. "Okay, fine. I still have a Google alert on him."

Penny groaned. "Oh my God. He's engaged to some actress or something. I don't know, she seems like she's a gold digger who just wants her princess crown."

"Yeah. But you know, ever since the whole Ashton thing, Roland's part of the family has been laying very, very low. They weren't exactly exiled, but they've sort of all self-exiled. They've kept low profiles, but the real truth is the Regents Council thinks it looks bad to have them around. So they're not *officially* exiled, but still, they're not exactly welcome back at the palace." I shrugged. "I mean it makes sense. Ashton was part of the conspiracy. They can't appear to favor them in any way."

"But it's not fair. I mean Uncle Roland abdicated the throne. His wife, well, that was a whole other thing. And I guess the whole Robert thing even makes it worse."

"I know, right? So basically, Tristan is never coming back, which is fine because then I don't have to see him."

"Oh, honey. I wish you would have told me."

"Well, it doesn't matter now. I never have to see him again, so it'll be fine. I'm over it anyway."

Of all the things I'd said today, that was the one thing Penny let me get away with. Because deep down, we both knew it was a lie.

Chapter fifteen

NEELA

"**P**lease tell me you have shagged your hot manny."

"No Bex, I have not shagged the hot manny."

Bex yelled over her shoulder. "Pay up."

"Seriously? You two are taking bets on me?"

"Yeah."

Adam yelled back, "She made me."

I rolled my eyes. "You two are impossible."

She grinned. "Oh we know."

"Whatever. I'm going to start some initial inventory at the gallery. I'm also going to see if I can find any damn clues about the ledger Willa gave me. Hold down the fort?"

"Okay. You have fun now and remember, a well-shagged boss is a happy boss."

I shook my head as I let myself into the house. To my

surprise Ariel was there going over some things with Jax. "Oh, Ariel. I didn't expect you."

She smiled, and I was once again reminded that every single one of these nannies was superhot. "Yeah, kind of impromptu. I'm going over the new schedule with Jax. You look like you're headed out."

She was saying words, but I was too busy watching the way Jax's jeans fit over his ass. As he leaned on the table, his triceps looked ridiculous. Like he could plant himself above a woman and stay there for hours.

Oh hell. I dragged my attention back to her and what she was saying. "...I'd totally love to tag along if you don't mind. I just love that avant-guard stuff, and she repped an artist that I just love."

Wait, what? I'd been so busy staring at Jax's ass and triceps, I'd missed what she was saying. "Oh, uhm. I'm sure it'll be boring, but you can totally tag along. I'm afraid I don't know much about art, so I'll welcome your company."

"Oh, that would be awesome. I can drive too, so you can work if that's easier. Matter of fact, let me go get the car."

Wow, she was so helpful. I could totally get used to this having extra help around thing. "Sure. That works."

Jax turned, and his azure gaze met mine. "Is there anything in particular you want for dinner? I can get it prepped while you're out."

Christ the man was perfect. Why did he have to work for me again? "Tricep would be great." There was a beat of silence, then another. Christ, had I said tricep? "Sorry. I meant tri-tip. I think I saw some in the fridge right? And it should be simple to prepare."

He grinned and crossed his arms. Almost like he knew that I'd been ogling him like a horny, lonely old maid. "You got it.

Anything you need, just ask."

Orgasms. Are those on the menu?

Before I could say anything else stupid, I headed out of the house after Ariel.

The drive was mostly quiet. And it helped that I could work on the way there. I liked Ariel. She was no-nonsense, and there was something genuine about her. "I appreciate the company."

"No worries. I'm a total art buff so this is a treat. And Jax is busy with the baby."

"Right. He's been a big help. It's taken some getting used to having to think of the little person all the time."

"Of course. Most people have plenty of time to think about it. Even if they're adopting, they still have done nothing but think about having a small person around. She just showed up in your life, so of course, it's taking some time."

"No kidding, I have no idea what I would have done without Jax." Fuck, I was going to sound like one of those horny moms. "All of you really. You all are heaven-sent."

Her smile was warm. "He's great with kids. I'm convinced he's a big kid himself."

"I wouldn't be surprised." Do not do it, do not pump her for informa— "So, what's his deal? He's seriously too good-looking to be let loose on the world."

She rolled her eyes. "Please don't tell him that. I don't think his head could swell anymore." She laughed. "He's a good egg though. A bad breakup messed him up, so he's finding his feet again, I guess."

"Who's the crazy woman who let him go?" Stop it. You might as well wave a flag that says *I want to shag your employee.*

"I know, right? He's not my type, but even I can see he's easy on the eyes and loyal to a fault." She studied me as I turned off the alarm at the gallery. "What about you? What's your story?"

Shit. "Oh, I'm not interested. I'm not trying to do your employee or anything." *Liar*. "Just curious. Someone like him should have family."

Ariel didn't even try to hide her smile. "Nice attempt at deflection."

I laughed. "I had a bad breakup too, but I'm not looking. I have to get my company stable and take care of Mayzie, and he works for me, which would be inappropriate."

"Uh-huh. But you should date. I hear it's good for the soul."

"Do you subscribe to that?"

She shook her head, sending her hair cascading around her shoulders. "Nope. But do as I say and not as I do."

I laughed. "So anyway, I just wanted to check the gallery because I got an odd call yesterday about a missing piece of inventory, and I haven't been able to shake it lose."

Her dark brows drew down over green eyes. "What kind of call?"

"Oh, nothing major, just a client who didn't get a delivery. The delivery of the vase they purchased was supposed to have happened the same day that Willa died. And according to her inventory system, it was delivered that day. I can't shake it, so I figured maybe I'd come in, look in the back, and see if there was anything that said, you know, 'hidden vases here.'"

Ariel chuckled. "Well, I'm glad you didn't mind me coming with you. Let's have a look."

I used the PIN code I'd been given to unlock the inner door. Everything opened, and the alarm system chimed, and I typed in that password as well. All the lights flickered on, shining on the bright white marble floor.

I'd always loved the gallery. Willa always had the most beautiful pieces displayed. Every time I entered, I felt like I was transported into this whole other world that I only got to visit from time to time. A world of beauty and excellence.

But now the walls were bare, and the cabinets were empty. I led the way to the back, and Ariel followed. Her shoes barely made any sound on the floor. She was wearing some kind of ballet flat, but it looked somewhat like a runner's racing flat.

Back in the day, Willa and I had been on the track team. I ran middle distances, and I'd had racing flats that looked a lot like that. Designed to not make any sound and be light as air.

There was another PIN code for the inventory room. And when I clicked that door open, I realized that it was actually the majority of the building. "Wow, okay, so where does one find vases?"

"Well, I have no idea. I mean, is it like some super old antique thing, or what?"

I shook my head. "No, Willa dealt in modern art. And this particular artist is still creating."

It took us twenty minutes before we finally found where the vases were. They were all dated and named. Ordered alphabetically. But the one I was looking for wasn't there.

I shook my head. "It's not here, so it must have been delivered."

"Do you have any reason to think it *wouldn't* have been delivered?" Ariel asked.

"No. But the client seems so sure, you know?"

"Well, maybe someone else signed for it. But that's on him, not you. Come on. Some of these pieces are beautiful, but my arachnid senses are giving me the let's-get-moving vibe."

We marched out and I locked up behind us. I would have to decide what to do with the gallery space. There were so many pieces in there. But it was part of Mayzie's legacy, so I would have to hire someone to manage it if I wanted to keep it for her.

As soon as we were back in the main gallery, Ariel stepped in front of me and shoved me back so quickly I blinked.

And what do you know, for such a little thing, Ariel was strong. She shoved me so hard, my shoulder blades hurt from where they hit the wall. "Ouch."

A woman called out, "Willa?"

Ariel pressed a finger to her lips to indicate we needed to be quiet. Why the hell wasn't she freaked out? Then she stepped out around the corner first.

There was a shriek. "Oh my God! Oh my God! Thief. Someone has a gun."

I poked my head around the corner. Then I rolled my eyes. Jane was always overly dramatic. "Jesus Christ, Jane. Ariel, this is Jane MacKenzie. Jane, this is Ariel, she's a friend and runs a nanny service."

Jane clutched her purse to her chest and continued to yell. She hadn't even heard me.

I thought I'd feel more... something... seeing the woman who had helped raise me. But all I felt was numb. I hadn't seen her much after I left her house, not even at my graduation.

"I will call the police. Who do you think you are? Breaking in here with a—" She stopped short when she finally noticed me. "Neela? What in the hell are you doing here? I guess you and Willa finally made up?"

She didn't know? Was I going to be the one who had to tell her? She'd always been resentful about taking me in. I'd always felt unwanted in her house.

But I'd been the daughter she always wished she had. I'd been the one focused on school and not boys. I never got into any trouble. Mostly I'd wanted to be as invisible as possible. Basically, Willa and I had been total opposites.

When I couldn't find my voice, Ariel spoke for me. "I'm sorry, ma'am. Willa isn't here. There is something you should know."

The older woman frowned. She was the spitting image of how Willa would have looked when she got older. And their personalities were quite similar too. Except Willa had a good-hearted streak of kindness in her that she just rarely displayed. Mrs. MacKenzie, on the other hand, lacked that genuine goodness.

"What do you mean? What are you people doing in Willa's gallery? Are you finally showing your true colors and stealing from her?"

I would never know why this woman hated me so much. But her hatred helped me find my words. "Actually, I'm managing the gallery now."

She frowned. "What do you mean?"

I inhaled sharply and released my breath slowly. How was her relationship with her own daughter so estranged that no one had notified her as Willa's next of kin?

"Mrs. MacKenzie, Willa died in a car accident almost two weeks ago."

The older woman blinked at me and stepped back several feet. "You're lying."

"No. I'm afraid I'm not. Her lawyer, Dan Bipps, is handling the paperwork. Willa was quite specific. She didn't want a funeral. Just her ashes spread. I was only notified because I was listed as guardian for Mayzie."

It had been a while since I'd seen a legitimate hissy fit from an adult. Sure, I saw them from Mayzie all the time, but Mayzie was a baby. This woman was grown.

It started with the denial head shake. And then the stuttered repetition of, "No. No, no, no, no, no." And then the lunging for me. Ariel was surprisingly quick and stepped in front of me, taking the brunt of the attack. The poor girl wasn't even caught up in any of this.

And then came the anger. "My daughter would *never* have left everything to you. She knew you were always jealous of her."

"I'm so sorry, Mrs. MacKenzie. I assumed Mr. Bipps had contacted you since you are her family."

"You're lying. This is a lie. Where is my granddaughter? Someone would have notified me to take care of her."

I shifted uncomfortably on my feet. "Just call Dan Bipps. He's been her solicitor for years."

"This is a lie. My Willa is coming back."

Over her shoulder Ariel winced.

"No, Jane. I'm afraid she's not."

Chapter sixteen

JAX

From the hallway, all I could hear was, "Ow, ow, ow, ow, ow, ow."

When I ran to the upstairs balcony, Neela had the ledger out and she was trying to stand. But she was caught somewhere between sitting and pulling herself up to the railing. "You need help?"

Of course, she was mule-headed, so she said, "Nope. Got it. I'm fine. Go to bed."

Luckily, I knew better now and ignored her. I jogged over, wrapped my arms around her waist, and helped pull her to standing. "What's wrong? Are you hurt?"

"No, I'm not hurt. I just—"

"It's a lot easier if you don't try and pretend. It's a lot easier if you just tell me the truth. And that way I can fix it."

"I don't need you to *fix* anything."

I glowered down at her with a raised brow. She chewed her bottom lip. "Okay fine. It's my neck. And the way I've been sitting is sending radiating pain down my back."

I grinned. "So, your neck and your back?" I could almost hear the song in my head.

She blinked up at me innocently, but I saw her lip twitch. She was well aware of the song too.

"It's fine. I, um—" She tried to extricate herself.

"Oh, you're not going anywhere."

"Jax, it's fine. You don't have to, you know, manny me or whatever."

I laughed. "What does that even mean?"

"I see you do it with Mayzie. Where you give that stern, authoritative look. And then you do the one thing she doesn't want you to do, and somehow she's all happy about it." She crossed her arms. "Can't make me feel that way."

I grinned. "How about we make a bet?"

"Why do I get the impression I'm about to make a Faustian bargain here?"

I shrugged. That was because she was. "I'll help you with whatever pain you have, and you tell me something about you. Growing up."

She frowned. "What will I get , you know, when you're not able to fix me?"

Good thing we never had to get to that point. "I know how to fix everything."

I gently turned her back around so she was looking out over the grounds and into the distance at the water.

"Why are you so... sure of yourself?"

I had to laugh. "Part of me thinks that maybe you were going to say something other than sure of myself."

"Okay, yeah, I was going to say cocky."

I leaned forward. My lips almost against the shell of her ear. "You haven't seen me cocky, yet."

Fuck, I was turning myself on. Or maybe it was her scent. I thought of a dozen ways I could plant her hands on the railing, kick her legs apart, lift up her skirt and sink deep. There was no one here now. I could have her begging for me in less than a minute.

Oh, God, even better. Legs spread, me kneeling behind her, licking.

Yes. Much better.

"Jax?"

I shook my head and blinked. "Yeah?"

"Where'd you go, I thought you were the one who insisted on this massage, you know, my neck and my back."

I couldn't help it, I finished the line for her. "Your pussy and your crack?"

She choked out a laugh. "God, that song's the worst. Every now and again Bex will start humming it in the office and it's like the worst ear worm. You can't ever get it out of your head."

"Back in London they made a drum and bass version of that song. It's actually really good. But when you hear it, you'll find you're singing it to yourself for days on end."

"I don't need to hear any other version of that song. It's bad enough when Bex does it."

"Come here." I reached for her. Sliding my hands over her shoulders. God, I wanted to touch so much more.

"No, it's fine, honestly. You don't have to." Her shoulders were stiff, and she clearly was uncomfortable with me touching her.

"If you don't want me to touch you, I won't. I'll only do what you want me to do."

Stop talking like you're having sex with her.

It wasn't my fault. That was just my voice. It also happened to be the same voice I used when I was having sex, but that was hardly the point.

She cleared her throat. "No, I just…" She turned slightly and gasped. "Oh my God, okay, yeah, please help me. I'll behave."

"Was that so hard?"

She shuddered and winced at the same time.

Then I worked, sliding my thumb along her neck, all the way to the top of her shoulder and bent down until I hit that little knot next to her shoulder blade. My touch was light. I didn't apply much pressure at first.

I wanted her to relax. To get used to me touching her. To feel good with me touching her.

Dick: *Mate, can we move this along? Because I'm about to turn blue if you don't do something.*

I wasn't listening to him. This was about a massage. Making *her* feel good.

Dick: *I have lots of ways of making her feel good.*

Again, ignore. Nothing to see here, folks.

Dick: *Except a really big me.*

I almost choked on my own joke. Instead, I gently massaged. Only applying more pressure once she was more insistent.

"Oh my God. You are magic with your hands. What the hell are you doing to me?"

"Just loosening those knots. You're going have to change the posture of how you work."

"I know. I don't normally work on my couch. That's not usually how I roll, but with this stupid ledger, I'm not able to work on it during the day, so at night I come and sit on the couch and try to figure it out. Clearly, that's not working well."

"Still don't know what it is?"

"No. I'm starting to feel like I'm not as smart as I thought."

"Something tells me you're smarter."

I was leaning over her now, and I was sure my breath was on the column of her throat. If I wasn't careful she was going to notice the hard ridge of my erection.

"Come on, tell me about growing up. It'll help relax you."

"I hardly think so."

"Come on. You're already feeling better, which means I'm already winning this bet."

"You know what, there would have been a time that you wouldn't have even known the level of my petty until it smacked you in the face."

I chuckled. "Come on, just tell me."

"Let's see, my dad. He used to make these puzzles all the time for me to figure out, and he'd leave them places for me to find, a little hidden treasure chest. I didn't recognize he was trying to make me smarter at the time. I guess but it was for the best. I always felt cherished and loved and had this great sense of satisfaction when I finally was able to solve the puzzle. Even though he knew things were hard for me with my mom gone, he always wanted me to have something that was just us, regardless of what was going on. But then he was gone too. He died when I was eight."

Fuck. "Sorry."

She shrugged. "I turned out ok. I might not have had a lot of time with him, but it was quality time."

"You said things weren't easy for you growing up? Before he died."

"Oh, he was always working on these high-profile projects. International spy stuff, you know. Took him traveling a lot. When he could, he'd take me, but there was always an armed guard around." She shook her head. "As an adult I see they were there for his security, but they terrified me as a child. I might do what my father did, but he always wanted a simpler life. I wanted that for me too. Simple. I guess things have gotten a little complicated now, but I don't want Mayzie to grow up like I did... afraid all the time."

You are an asshole. I swallowed hard. "She won't." The lie burned as I swallowed it.

She changed the subject. "What about you? Who was Jax Reynolds as a little kid?"

I frowned at that. "I don't know, I was a handful. Driven. I wanted to do well. But I had the tendency sometimes to get into trouble."

"What, you, trouble? I doubt it."

I hit another knot. And this time I did press hard, I applied more pressure with both my thumbs. She gasped. But the way she was standing, she was bracketed by my hips. "Relax. It will only hurt at first. Then it'll feel good. Just feel how I'm pushing in a way to dissipate."

"That is, magic."

"No not magic. Physical therapy. You should probably be getting more massages. And if that pain is a stress response, you have to find out how to reduce that."

"I think you just reduced it for me."

"Well, while I am perfectly happy to be your de-stressor at all times, I do have a baby to watch. So you're gonna have to figure out how to not let this happen again."

Because if I ever put my hands on her again, I was stripping her naked. That was just the end of that.

She rolled her shoulder. "Thank you. I don't even know what to say."

"You don't have to say anything. When I told you I was here for you, I didn't just mean Mayzie. I really am here for the both of you."

"You know, you're bossy, but you have your good points."

I grinned at her. "Sweetheart, you haven't even seen bossy yet." Better I ease her into that idea. "If there is something you need, but you can't find a way, the whole point is you're supposed to call me. I'll take care of everything."

She turned around slowly in my arms, licking her lips, her gaze falling on mine. It looked like she wanted to ask me something, and chances were it was inappropriate. So it was best we didn't go down that path.

Because if she makes another innuendo joke, you're not gonna be able to let her go. And you'll show her just how bossy you are.

"Well, thank you, you have made my life so much easier. And thank you for the massage too."

I nodded slowly. "Go on and get some rest."

"Is that you telling me what to do again?"

I grinned. "Absolutely not. It's merely a strong suggestion."

NEELA

I was burning both ends against the middle. My company was on steadier ground now that I'd moved us to the guesthouse and cut expenses. It was alarming the things Richard had been spending money on.

The last couple of weeks I'd started to get a handle on things again, which was surprising given everything that was going on.

Adam and Bex were more than pulling their weight, and there was a light at the end of the tunnel. But I wasn't out of the woods yet. I still had a lot of work to do.

And I had that journal to crack, but I couldn't afford to get preoccupied with anything right now.

The problem was all the other areas of my life were winding down a shit spiral.

The gallery was one thing. I'd have to hire someone to catalog all the pieces then get someone to put together a show. It was all well and good to have expensive pieces in a private collection, but they couldn't just sit. Could they? Willa had obviously left plenty of money for Mayzie, so maybe they just could.

But there had to be artists waiting to have their pieces shown. I wouldn't know until I had someone catalog everything. The inventory records were complete, but someone needed to make sure everything was accounted for.

I'd already spent the previous day trying to chase down a missing vase. And another client had called about a missing painting that was also supposed to have been delivered that Friday when Willa died.

I had to call Dan Bipps to see if he had a lawyer that could handle these matters. Since I'd been named to take over as trustee of her estate in a year's time, I felt like it was my responsibility. But I hadn't made promises I couldn't keep. I didn't know what happened to their art. All I knew was that I didn't have it.

And last night, Mayzie hadn't slept. *At all.* Every two hours she'd woken up screeching the house down. But when I ran in to check on her, Jax was already there.

This morning, he looked as haggard as I felt. Eyes red, but also happy to hold the baby. Once during the night, I'd walked in to find him completely shirtless, which was... good grief. That man was dangerous. Super dangerous. He shouldn't be walking around shirtless or someone could spy that intricate shoulder tattoo, or you know, lick his abs. He'd turned around confused, as if surprised to find me there. He held her sweetly, calming her down. "Is she teething?"

He nodded. "Yeah, the stuff I rubbed on her teeth wears

off after a couple of hours, and she wakes up pretty pissed off about it. Don't you, Mayzie? You don't like your gums hurting, huh?"

The way he crooned to the baby was as if he was meant to do that. Absolutely *meant* to be a father. Or in this case, a manny.

He's not your manny to keep.

That morning we were both silent, exhausted, and Mayzie was still cranky.

And after that, I'd had the day from hell. There was another missing painting, a client that wanted a complete change in scope, and I walked in the house to find Mayzie screeching her head off, again.

I went straight to her, but when I got within a step of her, she threw her block at me.

I stared down at it, my own tears welling from frustration and exhaustion.

Jax knelt by her immediately. His voice was low, gentle, but admonishing. "Mayzie, love. That's unacceptable behavior. We do not throw things at Mommy."

Mayzie blinked her teary eyes several times, wailing even more. She hadn't expected that he would scold her. Not that he was even yelling. But he never used a stern voice with her.

He picked her up, carried her to the corner of the kitchen, and sat her on the little stool. "Everyone needs a time out."

Cue the 'I'm dying' wailing. It was as if he'd spanked her.

All I could do was stare at the little green block on the floor. Jax walked over to me. Gently he rubbed my lower back. "Are you okay?"

"Of course, I'm okay. She's a baby. I just—it's been a day."

Much like my new daughter, I felt like wailing too. That thing in my upper nasal cavity prickled and warned me that tears were imminent if I couldn't get myself together. "I just don't know what to do. I am failing at everything right now, and Mayzie throwing blocks at me just seems like extra icing on this shit cake."

His voice was firmer as he continued to ignore her crying. "She's a baby. She's going to throw things. You can't take it personally. Just like you don't take the poop personally, except for that time after Mommy and Me. It was like she reached for me deliberately so she could poop in my arms. But I digress."

My lips twitched. What was it about him that could put me at ease and immediately take my mind off of everything?

"I just—I can't fail at this too, you know? My whole life, I have liked order and things that are nice and neat. Obviously, having a baby is very different. It's not even like I never wanted babies, I just haven't really had the time or my ideal partner. And now that I do have a baby, all she does is screech at me."

"That's all you're seeing right now because she's upset and her teeth hurt. She doesn't know how to channel pain, so she's going to scream.

Go on. upstairs, with you. Take a shower, and I'll bring you a glass of wine."

"Bossy."

His smile was wry. "I know."

I tried to fight his commands. "No, I need to figure out dinner."

He leveled his gaze on me calmly. "*No*. You're having a bath. I fed Mayzie and gave her a bath already. I just had her down here so she could see you before she went to bed. Is this the time you want to argue with me?"

I was too tired to fight. "Fine. But only because I'm exhausted."

The tears were dangerously close, so I walked over to the

corner and kissed Mayzie on the forehead. And then I bolted. I was going to the shower to cry in peace, and then I'd feel much better.

Famous last words.

JAX

I laid the baby down. She was still fussing, but she found her thumb and was sucking on it. Poor little thing. "I know the gums hurt, love. I've put medicine on it, so you can get some sleep, okay? How about you let your mummy get some rest, yeah? And me too? It would be bloody brilliant."

I was knackered. I needed the little angel to sleep. First so I could catch some sleep, but also because I needed to finish up the research into Neela's ex. I hadn't had much time during the day because the little angel was in a right mood.

We were short staffed. Ariel was jumping in where she could, and we had two new team members being recruited, but having no time off from the little one was difficult.

Are you sure no time off from your boss isn't the problem?

Not that I particularly wanted time off from her, but being this close all the time was making me just a little obsessed with her. Her no nonsense stride, her complete business-like efficiency with her body. Nothing wasted. Nothing stiff. Somehow fluid like a dancer.

I could smell her through the house. The honey and lime scent was unique to her. The little one mostly smelled like baby and nappies. But Neela … her scent might as well lure me to the rocks like a siren's call.

When she'd been about to lose it and start crying, I could tell all she needed was a moment. And honestly, Mayzie was having a moment of her own. Her teeth hurt. She hadn't been sleeping. She really wanted a biscotti. And while it might feel good on her teeth, it wasn't particularly healthy.

I'd given up and given it to her. But when I did, she threw it at me. She'd had enough, but at least she was finally resting.

I could hear the shower going as I charged up the stairs with the wine. I already knew the layout of all the rooms upstairs, and with the shower going the door would be closed, and I could just shuffle into the bedroom and leave the wine on the bedside table. Easy peasy. I knocked softly, just in case she was in the bedroom. But there was no sound, so I walked in and deposited the wine as promised.

She'd feel better after a drink. And maybe I could get her to tell me what was going on. From the sounds of it, there were problems with the gallery. From what I'd seen of Willa MacKenzie's financials, there was no way she was raking in that kind of money with art alone. I'd never met the woman, but I hated her already for pulling her unsuspecting friend and the beautiful baby that deserved better into some kind of shady dealings.

I strained to hear if maybe Neela was one of those people who sang in the shower, but she wasn't. It was silent, and I quietly exited the room, turning around softly so as to not alarm her. When I whipped back around to walk back down the hall, my body slammed into something soft. Warm. Slippery and wet.

And my dick was all about it.

"Oh my God." She scrambled for the towel as she fell backward. I scrambled for her. I caught her easily, rolling us both as she landed on top of me. But that meant my hands were on her naked, well, arse. I put the towel onto her back. "Sorry." I averted my gaze and deliberately looked anywhere but at her.

"What are you doing in my bedroom?"

"I was leaving you a glass of wine."

"Oh. There were no towels. I guess the cleaning crew came and they moved everything to the pantry, even though I left a stack in my bathroom. There were no towels in there, so I ran to get one, and I didn't think you'd come upstairs…"

I could do this. I could gently roll her over, grab one of the towels, and cover her body. Easy. I could do that. The problem was now I knew what she felt like, and as quick as the glance had been, I knew exactly what she looked like naked. In that split second, I had cataloged every mole, every freckle, the muscles of her abdomen, how high her breasts were, and the curve of her hip. I'd memorized it all.

I cleared my throat. "Ahem, we're going to—I'm going to roll you over now. And then I'll get the towel and cover you."

She gasped. "I—I'm naked."

I couldn't help but laugh at that. "Yes. I did notice."

I didn't exactly mean to draw her attention to my raging hard on, but the moment she wiggled, she gasped again. "Oh!"

I licked my lips and squeezed my eyes shut. "I'm sorry. That is purely biological. You're just naked and wet. Fuck, sorry."

I was anything but sorry. Anything at all. I wanted her to know exactly how much I wanted her. I wanted her to know exactly what I felt like. I wanted her to picture me beneath her naked and get creative on exactly what she was going to do to me. I wanted it all.

Her hands that had been pressed flat against my chest now went to cover her face. "Oh my God! Oh my God! What is wrong with me?"

I chuckled low. "Well, there is nothing wrong with you. Trust me on that. You're perfect."

I meant to keep that light and fun, but she just kept moaning.

"First, I nearly stick your dick in my mouth by accident. Then I say the most inappropriate things around you. And now this. I swear to God, I'm not trying to sexually harass you. I'm just clumsy and unlucky."

"The last thing I feel is harassed, but I think you can tell that. So, towel?"

"Yes. Um, towel sounds good."

I reached for the one that had fallen closer to my arm. I grabbed that and then I expanded it to cover her butt. I brought her around so she could wrap it under her arms, but I realized that no matter what she did, I was going to catch an eye full the moment she sprang up.

"I'm not sure how this is going to work. Maybe if I roll over on top of you, then you can adjust the towel how you need without me seeing anything."

Her voice went high pitched. "Okay. Fine. Great."

I had to try not to laugh.

Gently, with one hand braced on her lower back and one on the back of her head, I rolled us to the side. And what do you know, my dick was lined right up to her heated center, and I could feel every inch of her. I couldn't help the moan. I really couldn't.

She adjusted her hips to get more comfortable, and of course, that brought those sweet lips into full contact with my dick. I hissed. She choked. "Oh my God! I swear to God, I'm not doing this on purpose."

"No, but I'm doing this on purpose. I've wanted it from the moment I saw you. So, if you don't want me to kiss you, now is the time to tell me."

Her eyes went wide and if possible darker. She didn't say anything, but she nodded slowly. She wanted me to kiss her. And I groaned. "Then you better hang on."

Chapter seventeen

NEELA

His lips were shockingly soft. I don't know what I had expected. Maybe that he'd be brutal, harsh. He was big, and he looked like he knew his way around a kiss. Like he knew his way around sex. He practically oozed it.

But the kiss was feather light. Explorative. As if silently asking for the permission that I'd already given him verbally.

I kissed him back, and he opened his eyes, meeting my gaze. The ice blue in his eyes picked up more color as if they were going darker. Those thick lashes lowered again, and the next kiss he gave me was one that said he meant it. He was more explorative and more, well, possessive.

His lips glided over mine, coaxing, insisting that I play along. Then his tongue slid into my mouth, licking inside, demanding that I respond, and I did. He moaned. I could feel the length of him pressing into me as if begging for entry. Instinctively, I raised my hips.

He growled. Before I knew what was happening, he was pushing away from me but still refusing to let go of my lips. He went to his knees and picked me up beneath him, his hands on my ass.

My bare ass.

He held me against him and I locked my legs behind his back. He turned us and placed my back against the wall. And then he unleashed pure sexual energy.

As his lips owned mine, I realized I had never been kissed like this in my life. The clash of teeth, lips, desperate hands roaming free.

His hair was silky soft, the places where it was cut short like the softest purr. I raked my nails through, and he shuddered. His hips rolled into me, hitting me just where I needed it.

With a groan, I tried to climb closer, but I wasn't in control. He had me easily. His hands kneaded my ass, holding me firmly, digging into my flesh, possessing me. He hitched me up higher, and I gave a low moan of approval as the ridge of his erection ran over my clit. "Jax…"

He tore his lips from mine, kissing along my cheek down the column of my throat. "Yeah?"

"Bed."

His chuckle was low. "Oh, we'll get there. Eventually."

Oh, Jesus. This was not a man who made love in bed. This was a man who *fucked* wherever it was damn well convenient.

And where the hell have you been my whole life?

Everything I'd ever done had been safe and convenient. But I didn't want safe and convenient. Not anymore. Not after tasting Jax Reynolds.

And then his lips went back on mine, and his hips bracketed me in position with his hands sliding up my torso. One sliding and caressing all the way up my side to my hair and then digging in at the root. The other, sliding up and cupping my breast, his thumb gently sweeping over my nipple. Oh my God.

I arched my back, needing more contact. "You're so fucking soft," He muttered against my lips.

"Jax…" I couldn't think. How could I string words together? Could I just pant and have him know to keep doing whatever the hell he wanted to do to my body?

He tore his lips from mine, kissing along my jaw, the hollow of my neck. "I've been so fucking desperate to get my hands on you."

And touch did. He kissed along my jaw. Nipping, sucking, licking my collarbone. I was on fucking fire, and he wouldn't put me out. He just kept stoking the fire, adding more accelerant.

"Oh my God." My mind spun. How was this happening?

Jax palmed me with one hand, while his lips wrapped around my other nipple, and I moaned.

He sucked, tugging deep. Jax released my breast, sucking the other nipple. He traced his hand down my belly to the juncture of my thighs. I wanted his touch all over me. My thighs were locked together, the tension coiling in me so tight.

"Open," he said in a guttural tone, more growl than actual words.

My head lolled back and forth as I tried to force my body to comply. "Jax," I breathed.

He growled. "Open, Neela. I'm going to make it feel so good."

"Please, please, please."

"Shh." Suck. "You want this?" Lick.

How could he ask such questions? I was melting. Couldn't he see me melting? "God, yes."

"I know. You just want to feel good. So open for me,

darling." While his words still carried a desperate raw edge, he softened his tone. "Please."

My legs shaking, adrenaline coursing through me, I did as he asked. He rewarded my compliance with the tease of his fingers over my clit.

The quick feathered slide of his fingers preceded his mouth kissing down my body. He slid his fingers deep inside, curlng them as he watched my response, his gaze meeting mine.

I was half-way to O-town, so I had no idea how I looked. But I supposed it didn't matter because, then he was sucking on my clit and I couldn't think about a damn thing. Suck. Suck. Lick. Slide and retreat of his fingers, pressing over the G-spot.

He was going to make me come. And it was going to be screaming and uncivilized, and I didn't give a shit who heard.

If he just... I arched my hips into his mouth. I wanted more. I *needed* more. I tried to get him to press harder, to give me just the touch that I needed to...

There was a buzzing. The door opened downstairs, and then there was a buzzing sound.

Actually, two buzzing sounds.

Jax tore his lips from my clit, panting. "Shit. Someone's in the house." Quickly but gently, he eased me back. "Get dressed."

His tone was harsh, brutal, and I hated it. Just like that, he'd gone from being on the verge of giving me a much-needed orgasm to ordering me around. "What's happening?"

"In the bedroom. Stay up here until I call you."

What the hell?

He moved so fast I barely even noticed he'd already gone. But then I was clutching the towel to me and doing as I was told.

I ran into the bedroom and put on underwear, some sweatpants, a bra and a T shirt. In case I had to run fast, I didn't want to do it braless.

I found my bag, grabbed my phone, and ran for Mayzie. Just as I was about to open the door, the phone buzzed in my hand. It was Jax.

"Yeah?"

"False alarm. Do you know a Jane MacKenzie?"

"Yeah. She's Willa's mother. I just saw her yesterday."

"Yeah, well, she's here, and she's insisting on seeing the baby."

"Oh my God. I'll be right down." I swear to God, that woman had kept me from having an orgasm. I was going to kill her myself.

But instead of coming up with a proper murder plan, I turned away from Mayzie's door and headed down the stairs.

JAX

Holy hell.

I couldn't think.

I couldn't breathe.

What the fuck were you thinking?

I hadn't been thinking. She'd been naked, under me, and smelling so... my dick swelled.

Yeah, not a good idea.

And going down on her in the upstairs hallway. That was a good idea?

I'd slipped.

You more than slipped. That was one hell of a slip. One that almost had me turning her around to face the wall, then my dick sliding home.

Dick: *Maybe next time you get her to slip, trip and fall on me?*

No. No. No. No. None of that. I had a plan. I was going to

get back to the Royal Guard, and screwing the client was definitely one of Ariel's no-nos. I forced myself to take another deep breath and then jogged down the stairs.

I would have preferred to have my weapon on me, but it was stashed in my bedside table. My other one was stashed in Mayzie's diaper bag. All I had was a knife strapped at my ankle, but luckily, the intruder was busy announcing herself. "Yoohoo! Neela, are you here? Your security let me in. I just—"

She stopped talking when she saw me. "Can I help you?"

"Who the hell are you? What, so Neela has just taken over my daughter's life? My granddaughter? Her house, her men?"

I raised a brow. "Oh, so you must be Mrs. MacKenzie?"

"Yes, Jane MacKenzie. Who the hell are you?"

"I'm Jax Reynolds. I'm Mayzie's nanny… manny… whatever."

Her brows popped. "What? She is letting a *man* look after my grandchild? I will have her ass. I don't know who you are or what kind of man you think you are, but you are not appropriate to watch my grandchild."

"I guarantee you ma'am, I'm well qualified. Let me call Neela." One quick call and Neela verified the old lady was who she said.

Behind me, I could hear Neela scrambling down the stairs. "Jane." She came tumbling past me. I almost had to catch her, but touching her was not a good idea. Luckily, she caught herself. "What are you doing here, Jane?" Neela asked.

"Well, you said I could come by and see the baby."

Neela shook her head. "I meant you could arrange a time with me when Mayzie would be awake. She's sleeping. It's eight o'clock at night."

Jane glared at her. "I can see my granddaughter whenever I please."

Before Neela caved, I stepped in. "No, you may not. Given the way her mother died and all the upheaval, we have to keep Mayzie on a strict schedule. You can see her during the day. She's awake from morning until eleven. Goes out for a two-hour nap. You could also visit between one and three. She goes down for another two-hour nap after that. Any of those available times will work. Eight o'clock at night does not work for Mayzie or her schedule."

Jane looked like she wanted to blow a gasket. Her face went red, and I could see her working her molars back and forth. And if human beings could actually have steam come out of their ears, that would be her.

"How dare you tell me what is appropriate for me and my granddaughter."

Neela stepped between us. "Jane, if you keep shouting, you will wake that baby. And you are not seeing her tonight. Do you understand?"

The older woman blinked at her as if she couldn't believe that Neela was standing up to her. What the hell was their relationship? I'd read in the files that Neela had been raised by the MacKenzies after her father's death, but I didn't look too closely into the details. Was there animosity there? It certainly didn't seem friendly.

"Why you ungrateful little b—"

Nope. Not acceptable. I stepped forward, placing myself between Neela and Jane. "That's enough. I promise you, you will become persona non grata if you don't watch your language toward Ms. Wellbrook. If this kind of behavior continues, I will have you blocked from the property."

She glowered at me, derision in her glare. "You'll what? Under what authority? You're just the manny." She leaned around me to raise a brow at Neela. "Clearly, you're screwing him, and on my beautiful baby's furniture, no less. Tell me young man, were you one of Willa's? Neela has always been one to take Willa's secondhand things, you know. From clothes to toys, to books, to boyfriends."

Behind me, I could feel her stiffen. "Jane, that's enough."

Jane laughed then. Straightening up, she added, "Oh, she didn't tell you? Willa had this boyfriend in high school. He was just a plaything for Willa, you understand? Girls will be girls and all that. But ooh… Neela was jealous. So jealous. When the two of them broke up, Neela dated him for a while. Not like Willa wanted her leftover scraps anyway."

I made a mental note to ask her about that later. "It doesn't matter. It's time for you to go."

"You can't just kick me out. This is my house."

Neela stepped around me. Damn it. Why wouldn't the girl stay put? "No. It's my house. And right now, you aren't welcome."

"Well, I never—"

Neela shook her head. "Yes, you did. If maybe you'd shown me an ounce of kindness when I lived with you, I'd be more inclined to let you stay the night, as you have clearly been drinking. But as it is, I'll call you a cab and you can wait for it outside the security gates down the hill."

Jane teetered backward. "What has gotten into you?"

"Nothing. I'm just finally standing up for myself. It's time for you to go. If you want to see Mayzie, you can make an appointment. But until then, goodnight."

It was bad that I wanted her even more now. That little spark of fire, the refusal to let someone else walk all over her, it was hot. Very fucking hot. And sure enough, all my blood just headed south.

I shook my head to clear it. Nope, not going to happen.

Instead, I marched around Jane to the door, opened it for her, and waited.

Jane sauntered out eventually, her shoulders stiff and straight, as if we'd been putting her out. But she was the one who was out of line. When I closed the door behind her, I immediately hit the intercom. "Hey guys, can you make sure Mrs. MacKenzie gets down the hill? She's clearly been drinking, so call her a cab. And in the future, she doesn't enter the property without an appointment."

The response was immediate. "Yes, we'll take care of it." And then I turned my attention to Neela. "Are you okay?"

She met my gaze levelly, straight on, direct, and then she drew in a shaky breath. "I don't think so. I'm going to go get that shower then go to bed and maybe just erase this whole day."

I swallowed hard because *I* was something she wanted to erase. What had happened upstairs, she wanted that out of her head.

That's for the best.

Sure, the best, but it still sucked. I'd lost my bloody marbles kissing her, touching her. Another ten seconds and I would have been shagging her up against the wall, oblivious to anyone that might have been in the house or anything else that was going on in the world. This was smart. Backing off was the best option because I had a plan, and touching Neela Wellbrook was only going to get in the way of that.

Chapter eighteen

NEELA

'd been about to embark on the most epic night of my life, and Jane had clam jammed me. *Maybe it's for the best.*

Jax had gone back to pretending as if none of that had happened, as if none of my world last night had been real. It was like that fifteen-minute span had been a complete anomaly or I'd imagined the whole thing. His smiles the next morning were at odds with my desires and also at odds with the face he gave when he had complete and total focus, the one that made him look like a stone-cold killer. Then he'd helped me feed Mayzie and sent me off to work.

It had become the routine now. Mayzie got to see me go to work and I got to kiss her goodbye. That morning, she even let me feed her, which was astonishing because normally, she threw food at me. I'd become accustomed to needing to wear a shower cap to feed the baby.

It was as if last night had never happened. As if I'd imagined the whole thing.

Even Mayzie was in a better mood, like I was in some alternate reality where only I could remember the bad, insane, bizarre things.

But if he could pretend, then so could I.

Before I was out the door, he called out, "Any meetings today?"

"I'm supposed to go to a lunch meeting. But Ariel said she'd pick me up."

"Okay. It might be one of our new guys. Ariel will let you know."

"Okay." Then with a smile, he was off to do his thing with the baby. No hug. No sly remark. No sexy nothings whispered in my ear. Just goodbye, have a good day. And I *wanted* to say something. I was desperate to say something, But I couldn't muster up the courage to speak despite my level of frustration. I couldn't find any words to say.

I was a wreck when I stepped into the office. Bex and Adam exchanged glances. It was Bex who was brave enough to say, "Are you okay, boss?"

"Yeah. Fine. Why wouldn't I be okay?"

She stood and followed me into my office. "Well, I don't know. You seem, uh, wound a little tight."

"I'm fine." Wound tight didn't even begin to scratch the surface. I was so frustrated I could scream. I want to call Jane and whack a club over her head. But likely, that would not solve my problem.

How was she supposed to know I'd been on the verge of an epic O-athon. I certainly hadn't appreciated the side looks she'd given me and Jax, but that was another problem for another day.

I marched into my office, attempting to close the door

behind me, but Bex was on my heels. "Come on, spill it. Obviously, something is upsetting you."

I tried to smooth my hair back, but a narrow curl or two had escaped. "No, I'm fine. Everything is *fine*."

"See, you already said that, so that leads me to believe that nothing is fine. Come on. Is something up with hot manny?"

I flopped into my chair. "Okay, so you know how yesterday was just... you know, a day."

She sat in the opposite chair and nodded, coffee at the ready, sipping slowly. "Yes."

"Well, when I got home, Mayzie was also having a day of her own. The poor little thing was teething. And before that at the gallery, I ran into Willa's mom. No one told her Willa was dead, so I had to tell her."

"Damn."

"I know, right? So, this morning, I need to call Bipps and find out what the hell happened. Why wasn't she notified? And then last night she turned up unannounced, wanting to see Mayzie."

Bex frowned. "Wait, she showed up unannounced and just demanded to see her granddaughter?"

"Yeah, pretty much."

"The granddaughter that she wasn't named guardian of?"

"Exactly."

Bex narrowed her gaze. "Maybe I'm inherently suspicious, but I say don't trust dear old grandma. Still, none of that should have you looking like you're walking on a tightrope and desperate to either fall off or hack the thing to shreds."

I swallowed hard. I could lie. Lying might be preferable. But no. Chances were Bex would be able to see through the lie and then pester me all day.

"Okay, fine. Before Jane showed up, Jax and I were uh... making out."

It was as if Bex was a slow-motion cartoon figure. Her jaw unhinged, and she slowly lowered her coffee cup as she gawked at me. "Holy mother of hell."

"I know."

"Wait, I was opening the office as you were leaving the main house. Why were there no sexy nothings being whispered at the door?"

"Well, we got interrupted by Jane, and then this morning, he acted like none of it happened. Like he'd been invaded by a pod person last night and he didn't remember a thing."

"Oh, no."

"Oh, yes. So I barely got any sleep, and I'm just in a crap mood. Sorry. I will try to keep my darkening storm clouds of doom away from you and Adam."

"Oh, honey. You don't have to worry about that. Besides, I know how to fix your problem."

"How is that?"

"You seduce him."

"Uh, I don't think so. Remember, I'm the girl who doesn't like to be seen. So the last thing on earth I want is to have to be the one to take the first step."

"You don't have to actually take the first step, but you've got to let him know you're available. He probably thinks that you're freaking out about all of this being a very bad idea."

"It is a bad idea."

"I know. I'm just saying. You might be giving off the 'this is a bad idea' and 'let's forget it all happened' vibe. You need to be giving out the 'Hey, can I have some Os before we give up' vibe. You know… a few-for-the-road kind of vibes."

I choked back a laugh. "Oh my God, but why? Why are you my friend?"

She shrugged. "Because you need someone to say

outrageous things to you, and your life would have been dreadfully boring without me. So, if you're going to seduce him, I need to make you some appointments. You know, waxing, shaving those brows, the whole thing."

She touched my brow line. "What the hell is wrong with my brows?"

"Um, they're fine. You wear them a little full, so you know, just a clean-up. And how about a fun pattern downstairs?"

"Oh my God, are people still doing that?"

"Well, we can go old school, you know, just take everything like you've been mugged. Or we can turn it into a landing strip. You know, that's sexy and elegant again, old-fashioned. Or you can have a fun design, like an arrow."

"You know what, let's go back to that, 'I'm not sure why we're friends' thing."

"Because who else would help you jump the bones of your manny?"

"You know what, you have a point." If I wanted something, I needed to go out and get it. I'd done it with the business, but I was too afraid to do it in my personal life. And where had that gotten me?

"Okay, what do I need to do?"

Chapter nineteen

ARIEL

Zia smacked her gum as she soaked her feet in the pedicure tub. "I mean, I can't believe what happened to Willa, you know. She was like a super close acquaintance of mine."

Next to her, Jane MacKenzie scowled at her nails. "She was so well loved. Everyone loved her. I should know. I was her mom."

I almost snorted when Zia widened her eyes. She batted those false lashes like a pro. "I am so, *so* sorry for your loss. I mean at least you have her gallery. Something to remember her by."

And cue the bomb. This was our best chance at getting information out of Jane if she was the one behind the attempt on Neela and the baby. It was unlikely, but we couldn't leave any stone unturned.

Jane sniffled and sneered at the poor blonde who was doing her pedicure. "There were so many people jealous of her. They just wanted what she had. She had more than one friend like that."

Zia tried hard for an understanding and compassionate face, but she mostly looked constipated. "Oh, wow. It's so hard, especially after someone dies. You never know who's being real."

"I know that girl Neela isn't being real. She tricked Willa into leaving her everything. She stole my daughter's life. My granddaughter, the house, her man."

Zia's mouth hung open as I watched from across the shop. "She stole her man?"

"Mind you, Willa was highly sought after. She had her choice of men. But I went over there to see my granddaughter the other night, and Neela wouldn't even let me see her. And she was there with some man. He was clearly out of her league, so he had to be one of Willa's cast-offs."

"Wow, you don't seem to like her."

Jane sniffed. "I never have. I mean her father was some bigtime government freelancer, but when he died, he didn't leave her with money for me to look after her. I mean there was some, but children are expensive. That girl has always been a burden."

"I mean you totally deserve to be paid back." Zia nodded and twirled her dark hair on her finger. "You could sue her for damages or something."

"I should. But first I have to find out how much she made Willa give her. Can you believe no one even told me Willa was dead?"

Shit. She was telling a perfect stranger that she hadn't been notified of her own daughter's death. Which meant chances were slim she had someone try to pull the two of them off the street. There'd been a chance that she had been faking her surprise at the gallery. But watching her with Zia... it was unlikely.

Back to the damn drawing board.

JAX

Why the hell was I nervous? I was just meeting an old mate.

But there was something about coming home, being back here. The number of times I had been at this pub were countless, but still...

Maybe you can't go home again. It feels different now.

Trevor Tatters was at the bar, his golden-boy good looks attracting female attention, of course. When I walked in, his gaze flickered up from the brunette he was talking to, and he grinned and stood immediately.

"Jax! You old dog. Where the hell have you been hiding yourself?"

A grin spread over my lips easily. "Tatters, mate, how have you been?"

He clapped my arm and pulled me in for a one-armed man hug. "You look good. London been treating you right?"

I winced. "Actually, I've been back for a couple of weeks now."

Cue the scowl. "Why the fuck am I just hearing from you now?"

I shrugged. "Long story. I see you guys have some company at the bar."

He chuckled. "What can I say? Ladies love me."

He grabbed his pint from the bar and waved me over to a table. "Pool table's all ready. Your drink is on its way."

I raised a brow. "My drink?"

"I know you're still drinking that shitty Guinness."

I threw my head back and groaned. "Guinness is not shitty. It's the best lager, mate."

He shook his head. "Nah, man, I like IPAs."

Gross. "Too hoppy."

"Man, you don't even know. All these breweries have opened here in the last six months. All the Yanks bringing their love for beer with them. It's like a paradise."

"You're living the life."

Once my drink arrived, he racked up the pool balls. "So, what brings you back? Is it for good?"

"Yeah, it's for a while anyway." Since I didn't know how exactly it was going to go with Ariel, better to keep my cards close to the vest.

"Mate, when I heard... I'm sorry."

I rolled my shoulders and applied chalk to my cue stick. "It's all right. I probably should have known better."

He laughed. "Oh man, you loved her. Nothing we could have said would have changed your mind."

"It's funny how shit looks with twenty-twenty vision."

"Ain't that the truth? You couldn't have known."

"Ah, but I could have. You know all that shit you ignore when you're having all that crazy hot sex? That's the shit you pay for later."

He laughed. "Yeah, mate, always. But you know, you seemed to love her."

"Yeah well, I gave up everything for her. So that wasn't a good idea."

He winced. "You miss it, do you?"

I leaned over to break. When the balls scattered, I glanced up at him. "Every damn day."

He shook his head. "I'm sure if you appeal to Ethan, you know, he'd understand. He'd make concessions."

I shook my head. "I don't know man. It might not be as easy as all that."

"Well, I mean, it's worth a shot. Things have been, I don't know, tense. It would be good to have a mate back."

I frowned. "What do you mean tense?"

Trevor sighed and then ran a hand through his hair. "Man, I guess you missed a good lot of the drama. Well, obviously, you were here when King Cassius died."

I winced at that. "Yeah." I'd been on duty that night. Not on the king though. But there wasn't a guard on duty who hadn't considered what would have happened if they had been the ones guarding the king.

"Then things got extra interesting when the Prince returned."

"Yeah, I was here for some of that. And then well, like a moron, I left."

"Well, things got hairy. Roone got shot at a couple of times."

"Yeah, I knew that much. Which was one of the reasons she-who-shall-not-be-named insisted I needed to leave the guard."

He shook his head. "That alone is bollocks. Because at that point, she knew what she was doing, and she still chose to ruin your life."

I could feel the fury rising in me, but I kept a lid on it. "I made the mistake. I made the choices. She didn't make me do anything."

"No, but she didn't tell you the truth."

"Yeah, that much is true."

"So anyway, things got really interesting when they found the lost princess."

I ran a hand through my hair. "Yeah. That's wild. I caught up with Roone for a bit right after I got back. But we didn't get into all of it. So they found her, and he went undercover?"

Trevor nodded. "You know those Intelligence types. Clandestine shit. The rest of us plebs, we're just happy to watch the palace and make sure no one important gets shot, you know?"

I raised my beer in salute to that. When it was Trevor's turn to shoot, he landed the seven in the corner pocket and then the two in the side pocket. I'd forgotten how good he was.

"So what are you working on now anyway?"

He shrugged. "I'm on King Sebastian's traveling team."

I grinned at him. "Oh, look at you, moving up in the world."

"I don't know about that, but I just got back from a trip."

I knew I couldn't ask where he'd gone or what he'd done. That was the way of the work. And probably what used to twist up she-who-shall-not-be-named the most, the inability to tell her half of what I did with my day. "That's cool man."

"So, what are you doing?"

"I now work for a company called Royal Elite."

Trevor choked. "Ariel's company?"

"Yeah. I didn't know you knew her that well."

"Ariel? Are you kidding? She's a fucking legend. She was one half of the team that found the king, she is basically a killer hacker, *and* she's one half of the team that was guarding the princess."

Ah, so that's how she knew Roone. "She offered me a job, so I took it."

Trevor leaned back and gave me a slow clap. "Man, you are a fucking tough one. You leave the Guard, which everyone would argue was a mistake. Your girlfriend was a tart who got knocked up by some other bloke. But you managed to land a choice private-sector job for a fucking living legend? Man, you took some knocks, but you sure as hell landed on your feet."

I shrugged. "I didn't realize she was a big deal."

"Man, what hole have you been living in? Ariel is legit the real deal. She's best friends with the queen. Everyone said that it was bullshit that she had to leave the Guard."

"What do you mean she *had* to leave?"

His brows popped. "You don't know?"

I shook my head. "Nah, man, remember, I've been in London. I'm completely out of it."

He laughed. "Oh, you missed out on all the good gossip. Well, it turns out her dad was part of the conspiracy against the king. I don't know how he got in with that lot, but he did."

I cursed under my breath. "What the fuck?"

"Exactly. When she found out, she tried to bring him in. And then he tried to kill the princess, so Ariel shot him."

I stared at him. "She killed her own father?"

He shook his head. "Nah, the motherfucker lived. He's in prison."

I whistled under my breath. "Jesus Christ!"

"Yeah, but you know, no felons in the family. That's the rule. So she left the Guard. And apparently, King Sebastian was displeased about it. I can only imagine. The queen is her best friend. It was a whole messy, ugly thing. Rumor is the king basically blessed her agency, helped her out, the whole thing."

I took a sip of my beer. "Huh, I didn't know all the details." That was probably why she was so sure she could get me back in the guard.

"See, you have lived nine fucking lives. You landed on your feet and don't even know anything about your benefactor."

"Yeah, honestly it was super quick. Since I got here, there's been a job. Undercover. So we didn't really have time to, you know, talk about our feelings and shit."

"Somehow, I can't imagine you ever talking about your feelings."

I grinned. "Good point."

"Man, you need to do your research though. She is basically the anointed one. With her connections, you must have a killer client roster."

"It's not bad." Immediately, a vision of Neela filled my mind, and sure enough, the blood headed exactly where I didn't want it to. "I was due for some good luck."

"Yeah, I see. So what kind of gig are you working on? You said bodyguard?"

"Yeah. I got the night off, so…"

"You're being mum because of the contract?"

"Sorry man, habit. But yeah, basically. The client inherited a fuck ton of money, and someone tried to grab her off the street, so cue needing a bodyguard." I kept it vague out of habit.

"What? Someone tried to grab her off the street. And I noticed how you said 'her.'"

I chuckled. "It's not like that, man."

He grinned and bumped my shoulder as he walked past to set up his next shot. "Oh, I have seen *The Bodyguard*. Whitney Houston and Kevin Costner, back in the day. It was a looking-no-touching situation. But I know how it gets all intense and hot."

He wasn't wrong. "Nope, not like that."

He frowned. "Oh mate, is she busted?"

"Busted? You want to know if she's ugly?" I shook my head. "No. Fuck, no."

"So then she's hot."

Fuck. I walked into that one. "I didn't say that. All I said is she's not busted. But she's got a kid, so…"

He winced. "Ahh, that's always a little complicated. But, hey man, spending alone time together, keeping her safe…"

"It's not like that, man, I swear."

"What is with you? You're not still hung up on what's-her-face, are you?"

"Nope." Way over that. Sort of over that. Oh, I was over her, but I was still harboring some of that pissed off feeling.

"So, you're being all well-behaved because of your moral obligations?"

"Man, she's a client."

"And? Do you recognize that the king and queen got together when she was his bodyguard? And then you also recognize that Roone got together with the princess that way?"

I shook my head. "Yeah, you know, somehow I don't think I can bend the rules like that. I am no prince."

He laughed. "You know, that's the truth."

"Arsehole."

Something about just being able to talk to him eased some of the tightness in my chest. Just because I wasn't part of this family anymore, didn't mean they weren't still my friends.

For the rest of the night we caught up a lot on what my old mates were up to, and their families who had married and had kids. I don't know why I avoided this for so long. Maybe coming home wasn't going to be the exact same as it used to be, but it didn't have to suck either. And especially with a line back into the palace, I might be able to have it all again.

When I drank the last of my beer, Trevor met my gaze. "Man, I'm serious though. You didn't deserve what happened."

"Thanks, mate."

"You just pick the ones that need a rescue. Maybe one day you can find a girl who doesn't need rescuing. That would be good for you."

He was smiling, but there was something serious about

what he said. Was I always looking for someone who needed me? Neela needed me.

No, Mayzie needs you. Neela is along for the ride. And she made it clear that she really didn't need me.

But I definitely needed her.

I shook my head. "I hear you. But whatever you're thinking, it's not happening."

He shrugged. "If you say so. But, from what little you said about the woman you're guarding, I can hear it in your voice. You like her. And she doesn't need you, huh?"

"She doesn't know she does."

He laughed. "Man, maybe she doesn't. But someone like that is good for you. It'll keep you on your toes, but you can't rescue everyone. Maybe, just maybe, you can be with someone and know she won't do you dirty like the other one."

It was always fascinating to me.

Trevor seemed all happy-go-lucky. Like he had not a care in the world. But every now and then he would drop something meaningful like that. See through the heart of it. See that part of my problem with Neela wasn't that I worked for her or that I was lying to her. The real crux of it was there was a part of me that didn't trust her. I also didn't trust my ability to see all that bad shit coming.

Not every woman is she-who-shall-not-be-named. Sometimes what you see is really what you get.

The problem was the more I liked Neela, the more likely it was she was going to feel betrayed.

And I knew from experience what a secret like that could do to someone.

NEELA

I stared down at myself. What in the hell was I thinking?

You were thinking that Bex was right. That maybe he's worried that you're his boss, so he thinks he overstepped the line.

God, I hoped that was right. I hadn't seen him all day. The other nanny, Tamsin, had been here. She'd told me that Jax would be back by nine. She'd volunteered to stay with me until Jax got back, but I still wasn't used to having people underfoot. How had Willa dealt with it?

I also got the distinct impression she really didn't want me to leave the house at all. I didn't have any intention of leaving the house, but still, did they think I was completely helpless?

I was all clear to do this. Then, why was I so scared?

Maybe because you're wearing Willa's lingerie that barely covers anything and you're intent on seducing your manny.

I was an idiot. I swore it would be the last time I listened to Bex.

My phone buzzed on my vanity. And sure enough, there she was, Bex. I answered. "This is a bad idea."

"I knew you were chickening out."

"Yes, because this is *insane*. How in the world am I supposed to seduce him? He kissed me and ran away. That tells me he doesn't want this. And, oh my God, Willa's lingerie has not a scrap of fabric on it." I tugged at the lace see-through bra. It made my boobs look awesome. But also, you could basically see my boobs through the lace.

"That's the point of lingerie. It's not actually *supposed* to cover anything."

I scrutinized myself in the mirror. Okay, the yoga was working, but the thong... my ass was the size of the main island. Luckily, it had a little cover-up thing, but again, it was see-through. "It covers nothing."

Bex laughed. "Oh my God, it sounds so hot. Take a selfie."

I coughed. "A what?"

"A selfie. Better yet, send *him* a selfie and tell him to come find you somewhere in the house."

"No! I will not do that. Those things last forever."

"You want it to last forever. Trust me. You want him to have that one for the spank bank for years."

"God, Bex, do you have to say things like spank bank?"

"Spank bank. Spank bank. Spank bank."

"Real mature."

"I mean, come on, Neela. You have spent your whole life trying to make yourself small and be as little bother to anyone as possible. It's time that you stepped front and center for once. Be the hot girl that you already are but just don't *know* you are. For once, take the goddamn stage. You already know he wants you. From what you said about that kiss, it was the hottest. So just be you. Take a picture. Send it to that man. If you're wearing Willa's lingerie, then *be* Willa for a night. Just pretend. You want him, don't you?"

I groaned. "Yes."

It wasn't just that. I liked feeling sexy and fun. I also liked feeling like a woman. For so long, I had just been Richard's partner. Like he didn't really see me. But Jax... he seemed like he saw me. But then he pulled back, so yeah.

"This just isn't me."

"That's it exactly. You are so used to making yourself small so that you're not a bother, you don't know how to stand up and just be you and own it. That's all you have to do. Hell, you could be wearing a head to toe muumuu, and those moments when you are shining through would still be unbelievably sexy. You don't need to wear see-through lingerie for that. He already thinks you're sexy. So that's already a win. You just have to ovary up and tell him what you want."

I swallowed hard. I really did love her. "Oh God, this feels insane, but you're right. I don't want to hide anymore. I don't want to pretend to be small to make someone else more comfortable."

"Yes. That's the ticket. You're gorgeous. If I had your ass, I would basically walk around naked all the time."

"Bex, you do have my ass."

Bex choked a laugh then. "What? You're insane. I have a boy's body. Barely any hips, barely any tits. The moment you start paying me more or I marry a billionaire, I'm getting my boobs done."

"You don't need your boobs done, Bex."

"Not something ungodly, right? Because I'm small, but a nice tasteful C-cup. Like a small C. Just to fit into clothes better."

"Well, if that will make you happy, the second we get in some more clients, you'll get a big bonus and you can go get your big fake tits."

"Pamela Anderson, here I come."

"Oh my God, I'm so nervous."

She laughed. "I know. Look, just stand back, okay? Send me a picture."

I laughed. "What? I'm not sending you a picture."

"Yeah, you have to practice your selfie game. Come on, get on the bed. Take the picture and send it to me."

"Oh my God, why do I do these things with you?"

"Because you love me, and I'm fun. And you know that my selfie game is strong. Have you seen my Facestagram? It's fantastic."

Her social media account was pretty amazing. Bex was gorgeous. Pixie like. She was cute and engaging. People loved her.

"Okay, okay. Fine."

I climbed on the bed, still wearing the ridiculous see-through wrap, tried to pose myself, and then took the picture.

I heard the chime on the phone, and then Bex laughed.

"Oh my God, stop with that face. Like, honestly, look at the camera like it's Jax, okay? And then arch your back a little, tits out. You have a great set, show it off. And holy crap, is that thing see-through?"

"Yes! You see my problem?"

"Yeah, it's hot."

I groaned. "I—You know what? I don't even know what to do with you."

She laughed. "Love me forever. Okay, take another one."

I tried to follow her instructions. Sent another one. Rinse, repeat. Finally, I sent her one that she approved of. "Yaaass! That's the one."

I laughed. "You know I'm not sending that to him, right?"

"Of course, you're not. Even though I told you to. That's why I'm doing it for you."

I sat up with a start. "What?"

"You forget, I have access to your chat account, the one that we're all on. I can log in as you."

"You wouldn't."

"Um, and by wouldn't, you mean already did?"

"Bex!"

"You weren't going to do it. And well, you look hot."

"I hate you."

"I love you too. Byyee!"

And she was off the phone. I quickly opened up my chat app. And sure enough, there was me, sending a holy hotness picture to Jax. So far, he hadn't checked it. Oh God, how did I erase it?

I pulled up a website on my laptop with quickness, trying to figure out how I could recall a message. Holy shit. There was no recalling it. No recall.

Okay, maybe if I could hack into his account, I could delete it before he ever saw it. Also, I had no idea what he might use for a password.

"Oh God, this is terrible." I was going to kill Bex. That was it. No more best friend. Best friend was going to die.

Because she did the thing that you couldn't.

I slapped my laptop shut and placed it on my bedside table. Oh my God! I clutched my phone to me. Okay, I just needed a glass of wine. Everything would be fine.

I kept checking the app to make sure he hadn't seen it yet, and he hadn't. So there was that. Maybe he wouldn't see it. Maybe I could just pretend the whole thing had never happened.

I went downstairs and into the kitchen, pouring myself a very generous glass of wine. I downed it in one fell swoop, and then I poured another. It was the wine from dinner the other night. It wasn't likely we were going to drink it again, so I drained it and went back to my room.

I checked again to see if he had seen his chat messages, but he hadn't. Okay. I would just wait for him to come home, and then I'd explain that Bex was playing a joke. Of course, that was totally fine. I could do this.

I climbed into bed and waited for him. God, I was tired.

I checked the clock again. 8:50. Where the hell was he?

Before I knew it, my eyes were drifting shut. But I could do this. I'd just wait for him and explain. It was all a big misunderstanding.

JAX

I passed the security gate, nodded at Ted, who was on duty, and asked him what time Tamsin had left. He told me, and I nodded, knowing it meant that Neela had probably been antsy and wanted the house to herself. So Tamsin had been watching the house from the street.

I might not have wanted the night off, but I certainly needed it. I felt more normal now. Less on edge. Luckily, with the rest of the team finally hired, rotations would be a lot easier. It was more and more difficult to be in the house with Neela.

Especially since you touched her.

I'd done a whole hell of a lot more than touch her.

There were not enough showers in the world to take care of the perpetual hard-ons I had around her. Those constant interruptions to my flow were the reason I'd started taking Mayzie to the park more. It was easier to be out of the house than smell her perfume everywhere. Or maybe that was her shampoo? That honey and lime scent, I might as well be watching porn or something, because every time I sniffed it, instant blood diversion to my dick.

It wasn't exactly conducive to doing my job, keeping Mayzie safe.

And Neela. Don't forget her.

As if I could.

You just had to have a taste, didn't you?

I scrubbed a hand over my face as I parked the car.

Chill. You can do this. Just go inside, go straight to bed. In the morning, wake up early, and get another grueling workout in.

Hopefully, I could exhaust myself into not wanting her.

Good luck with that.

I locked up the car, went to the front door, and typed in my code. All the lights downstairs were on dim, so I turned them off as I went. It was only when I hit the stairs that I checked my messages.

I froze with a foot hovering over the first step. Holy fuck. All the blood in my body went torpedoing south of my heart as it raced to keep up with the flow and into my dick as it woke the fuck up.

Jesus Christ.

The chat app she'd gotten us all on so that I could communicate with Adam and Bex had one message from her today. A photo.

A photo of her wearing a lace see-through outfit of some sort. Her olive tanned skin was on full display as she wore a red sheer bra-and-panty combination that made my mouth drier than the Sahara. The expression on her face said it all. 'I cannot wait to fuck you.'

Jesus…

I clamped my hand hard on the banister and took several deep breaths. That didn't help, because what I wanted, what I needed, was to taste her again, to be with her.

Didn't you just have this conversation?

Trevor had said it. I was that guy. Even when I knew something was a bad idea, if my brain thought I could fix it, I would commit to fixing it.

Difference is Neela doesn't need saving.

I knew this was a bad idea, but I wanted her. It didn't matter that I knew it was going to end in a disaster. She was the client.

You technically work for Bipps.

I was Mayzie's fucking manny, so that might get awkward.

The baby loves you and has no idea what's going on, and you're actually good with the kid.

Also, I was lying to her.

I waited for the rationalization that would help with that one, but it never came because it was the truth. There was no rationalization for that one. I was lying to her, and when she found out, she was going to feel betrayed. It was going to hurt. And the last thing I wanted to do was hurt her. She didn't deserve that.

Okay, then keep your hands to yourself if you can.

I took another step, but my damn dick just swelled again, pushing against the metal fly of my jeans and making me wince. *Down boy.*

I could do this. Maybe I could pretend I hadn't seen it.

Except the damn app had read receipts, so she would know.

I finally climbed the rest of the way upstairs, my dick protesting the entire time, knowing that I was going to go the Boy Scout route. Hell, what was wrong with me?

There is another way. You could tell her the truth.

Yeah, I could do that, except that wasn't the job. The job was undercover, so Ariel would skin me alive, which also meant there would be no getting back in the Royal Guard. So as much as I wanted her, I couldn't jeopardize that future.

I knew I couldn't see her with my dick like this. But what choice did I have?

I knocked quietly on her door, which was slightly ajar, but she didn't come to the door. I knocked again. Finally, I pushed it open slowly, and the first thing I saw were her feet. One over the other, delicately arched, her toes painted in multi colors of pink and purple. I smiled because Mayzie had been the one to pick the colors.

Her toe color choice didn't match that flimsy piece of nothing she was wearing, but that was the last thing I cared about. The next thing I saw was tanned, smooth legs that definitely deserved worshipping.

No, that's not why you're here.

I knocked again. But she didn't stir. And then I poked my head in, yeah, she was definitely still wearing lingerie. And she was also definitely... *asleep*.

My dick roared in protest as if practically begging me to wake her. But there was no way I was doing that. Instead, I grabbed the blanket at the end of the bed, and I gently pulled it over her. I also turned off the bedside lamp beside her and then forced myself to turn around and walk away.

Chapter Twenty

NEELA

I'll take awkward for $300, Alex.

Things with Jax were... fine. Totally fine. So fine we were exceptionally polite to each other. Never mind that he'd made it a distinct point *not* to touch me.

Just the idea of leaving the office and going into the main house was slightly nerve-racking. Matter of fact, I considered sleeping in the guesthouse. There was a bed and a bathroom after all.

When Bex was leaving, she glanced at the clock. "Aren't you usually at home by now?"

"I'm already home. You forget I live here."

She narrowed her gaze at me. "Are you avoiding the hot manny?"

"I'm not avoiding anyone. It's just less tense over here," I lied through my teeth.

She rolled her eyes. "Honey. You can't avoid the man. How will you ever get boned?"

"Yeah, no boning here. I promise you that."

"That is such a shame. Such a shame. Because clearly you could use a good boning. And he wants to be the one to give it to you."

"No, no he doesn't. *He's* avoiding *me. I'm* avoiding *him*. We've both bought property in avoidance city. Even Mayzie's noticing it. She'll lean over with her doll and have her doll give us kisses and then look at us expectantly like she expects us to kiss or something."

Bex choked out a laugh. "See, even the baby thinks you need a good kissing. She doesn't know about the other stuff."

"Bex, stop it."

She laughed and then set the mail on my desk. "I checked the mail for you from the PO box. It's quite the stack, so you'll want to go through it. Just from the top I can see most of it is for fuckface, so you'll be able to shred those."

"I still have to tell him."

"No, you don't. Because they may be addressed to fuckface, but the next line is the company, which you still retain the name of, so fuck him."

"Okay, Bex."

Bex had two speeds; off or raging lunatic. And when it came to Richard, it was raging lunatic. "Sorry. I just still think you deserved better."

"Okay, thanks. I guess I'll go home."

She gave me a wink. "Please, get boned or at least bust out your vibrator. I'm pretty sure that thing has dust on it. But if you wash it it's still usable."

I rolled my eyes and ignored her. She went out the front, and I locked the door behind her then went out the back and set the alarm. Old habits die hard. Everything was as it should be. I glanced back at the safe security of my office. I could stay there for the night and order food, but likely Jax would bring it out to me and I'd still have to see him. But the awkwardness I'd have to deal with would be for a much shorter time. I could catch my favorite shows on my laptop, and I wouldn't have to walk in the house.

But then you'd also miss kissing Mayzie's sweet cheeks goodnight.

I groaned. "Fine, I'll be a fucking adult."

With the mail in my arms, I trudged over to the main house. I didn't even need my key. I pushed the door right open. Lucky for me, Jax wasn't even downstairs.

The baby monitor told me he and Mayzie were upstairs and he was changing her. The low crooning sound of his voice washed over me like melted chocolate, and it made me clamp my thighs closer together. I knew from personal experience just how low that voice could go. The things it could say.

Lord, Bex was right. I needed to get laid. Or at the very least go a really solid round with the vibrator, because I could not go on like this.

I started sifting through the mail and then got engrossed. It was that easy. The mindless task blocked everything out. I didn't even notice anything else until that sexy-as-sin voice was right behind me. "Are you hungry? Do you want me to make you something?"

I jumped. "Jesus Christ. You scared me."

Mayzie clapped at my exaggerated movement.

"Well, you know I'm in the house, right?"

"Yes, I did. I just…" I shook my head. "Sorry, I just was engrossed and wasn't paying attention."

He studied me. He was still only a foot away from me and God, those eyes. The ice-blue. Direct and piercing. Jesus Christ. I clamped my thighs together again.

Nope. We are closed for business. He works for you. He is your manny. You need him. And he clearly doesn't want to bone you, so stop it.

He held out Mayzie to me, and I gratefully took her. "Hey, baby May."

She gave me a pseudo toothless grin. The little nublets of her bottom two teeth were still pushing their way through, but at least she was much happier. And she was so damn soft. The smell of her shampoo instantly comforted me. She held on tight, spreading drool along my neck as I held her. Gross, but also the most comforting thing in the world. For several moments as I held her, everything else shut down. Okay, now I got it. The reason that moms, even in their most tired states, run and have another baby immediately after their first one. They want more snuggles. For as long as humanly possible.

"Neela?"

I lifted my gaze to Jax. "Hmm?"

"Food? Are you hungry?"

Libido: *Hell, yes, mama is hungry!*

"Oh, uh, I was just going to order something."

He shook his head. "It's no trouble. I can make you something. I'm just going to toss something together for myself, and I'll leave some for lunch tomorrow."

Don't be petty because you're horny. Eat the man's food. "Okay. Has Mayzie eaten?"

He nodded. "Yeah, I'm just going to make dinner. Then I'll give her a bath and put her down."

I shook my head. And not just because I wanted to get the hell out of his presence before I did something stupid, but also because he deserved it. He'd been on eighteen-hour shifts, and well, I sort of wanted to give her a bath. "No, I'll do it. Consider yourself off for the night."

His gaze bore into me, and it looked like maybe he wanted to say something.

Something along the lines of 'Hey, put the baby down and I'll bone you against the wall.'

No, that wasn't what he was going to say. I knew better.

"Thanks. But I can do it."

"No. You've done enough."

Shit. That was not how I wanted to sound. And from the slight narrowing of his gaze and the way his eyes flickered to my lips, that was exactly how it sounded. "Neela..."

I didn't let him finish. "I'm going to take her up. Come on, baby May."

Mayzie started with her baby chatter, possibly telling me about her day. Block building and Sesame Street and all that good shit.

Giving her a bath helped soothe the frayed edges. Maybe it was the scent of her lavender shampoo that was meant to make her sleepy and calm. Instead it made me much, much calmer, which was good. Because I couldn't go back downstairs and grab the mail without some level of calm. When we were done, and my shirt was wet, I put Mayzie down and gave her kisses and turned on her animal mobile that doubled as a nightlight.

In her little sleep sack, she kicked her little feet and then plopped two fingers in her mouth and started sucking. Before I was even out the door, her eyes had started to drift shut. Man, to have it that easy.

I shut the door quietly behind me and then faced the doom of having to go back downstairs. Maybe he was in his room. He seemed to be working on something the last week or so, but he hadn't said anything about it. My brain immediately tried to unravel the puzzle that was Jax Reynolds. He didn't talk about himself much. Didn't say much about his past, save our early conversations before things got... awkward.

When I went downstairs, he was nowhere in sight. I sifted through the rest of the mail, set aside the ones that were for fuckface, as Bex called him, and put those by the door so I'd remember to take them back over to the office. Then I sifted through the ones that were addressed to me. Mostly solicitations. A couple from clients who still hadn't remembered that they were supposed to set up auto debit, so those were checks.

Yay, money. And there was one I didn't recognize. I slid that one open. There was no post mark.

The lines on the side of the page were clear and easy to read though.

Give it to us and we won't hurt the baby.

The sledgehammer to the sternum was swift and painful. The bottom fell out of my stomach, and all of a sudden, the air whooshed out of the room. My head spun, and I had to clutch onto the edge of the table to steady myself. But something else steadied me. Just his arms around me.

"Neela? What's the matter? Neela?" His voice was low, but steely.

"I... Oh God."

The bile rose up, and I had to swallow hard to keep it down. Instead I just handed him the letter.

He cursed under his breath, took it by the corner, and placed it down. "Hey, we're going to put that in a plastic bag and then give it to the police, okay?"

"Jesus Christ. What the hell do they want from me? I don't know what I've done."

Jax turned me in his arms and pulled me to his chest. He tucked me easily under his chin, his big body completely enveloping mine in his warmth. He smelled so good. Like musk and the outdoors. All I wanted to do was lean in and inhale deeply.

"We will fix this. Okay? We'll figure it out."

"How? My number one job is to protect that little girl, and I don't even know how I'm supposed to do that. This is dumb. I should have just taken Mr. Bipps up on his offer for a security team."

He swallowed hard. "You want a security team?"

"I don't *want* one. But after a letter like that, threatening Mayzie? I know I haven't got anything anyone would want, but shit, maybe Willa did and I just don't know about it."

He held me close and kissed my temple. "You're okay. For now, you're okay. And we'll deal with that letter in the morning. All right?"

He ran his hand up my back, pressing me closer to him. And I wrapped my arms around his waist and for once, just let myself be held.

I wasn't usually one for hugging or really having anyone touch me. Mostly because from the age of eight to college, nobody touched me for any loving reason.

The MacKenzies barely ever touched me. And if they did it was to move me out of the way for something. Usually Willa. There were no hugs, no pats on the shoulder, no high fives.

Willa hugged. But even that felt weird to me. She was always holding me or hanging on. It always felt a little like I was drowning when she did it. Almost like she was shoving me under.

Wasn't she though?

And then in college, sure, guys touched me. All the time. Usually because they wanted sex. But that was men... so it was expected.

But it was rare that I got comfort for comfort's sake.

The problem was my body wanted a whole different kind of comfort.

Jax's tone was low and crooning. He whispered things in my ear. Things I didn't necessarily understand. In some other language I didn't quite get. But they soothed me nonetheless.

Into his chest I mumbled, "What language is that?"

"It's Welsh. It's something my mother used to say to me whenever I was upset."

"What does it mean?"

He chuckled. "Loosely translated it means 'have a brandy and everything will be okay.'"

I chuckled. "I think I like your mother."

"You would have loved her."

I tipped my head back. "Oh shit, has she passed?"

He nodded slowly. "Yeah. Three years ago."

"I am so sorry. I didn't mean…"

He shook his head. "First, no, how could you have known? Second, stop. I'm comforting you. Not the other way around. Just take it. And third…"

His gaze flickered to my lips again. And self-consciously I licked them.

I knew he wasn't looking at them to kiss me. He'd already made it pretty clear he wasn't interested. Hadn't he?

JAX

I knew all the reasons this was a bad idea. I could list them.

I technically worked for her.

She made me want too much.

My control was already shot to hell.

Oh, and I was lying to her.

Fuck. Fuck. Fuck. I couldn't do this. "Neela—please don't

lick your lips like that. You're killing me." Jesus. Why did it sound like I was growling? Any moment now I was going to morph into a Neanderthal and toss her over my shoulder.

That doesn't sound so terrible.

Her lips twisted into a wry smile. "Why? You want to do it for me?"

My dick practically hummed. Asshole. "We can't. I haven't told you—"

She shook her head. "You make me feel all these things. For once, I don't want to think. I just want to give over and be present. Can we do that?"

Shit.

When I teased my tongue between her lips, she sighed as I licked into her mouth, stroking deep, turning up the temperature. I was so fucked. She was going to kill me.

She was very quickly becoming an addiction. With every taste I was falling further and further into the abyss.

Deepening the kiss, I angled her head so I could slide my tongue in deeper, tasting her more fully. Her lips were so soft. So perfect. I could kiss her for hours and never get bored. When she made a happy purring sound in the back of her throat, my blood hummed.

As I kissed her, I pressed my body into hers, needing to be in contact with as much of her as possible. I wanted to bury my cock deep inside her tight walls. All I'd dreamed about was pulling orgasm after orgasm out of her.

Muffling a curse, I lifted her and sat her on the countertop, stepping between her legs. A charge of electricity ran through me the moment my pajama-clad cock came into contact with her sweet center. All that separated them was the cotton of her shorts and my pajama bottoms.

She lifted her hips, bringing her core closer to me and I

groaned, not daring to stop. I *needed* her. And it scared the shit out of me. But I didn't dare stop. Wouldn't stop.

When Neela rolled her hips into me, my hips jerked. She was so responsive. I snuck my hands under her top and she sucked in a shuddering breath.

God, she was so bloody soft. It had been easy to imagine that I'd fabricated how soft she was, but I hadn't.

My thumbs skimmed up her ribcage and I could feel her holding her breath as I traversed each of her ribs. When I reached the underside of her breasts, a shudder rolled through her body.

I wanted her to need me as much as I needed her. Gently, I palmed her breasts. Her breathing shallowed, and she threw her head back. "Jax."

Jesus, fuck. Her breasts spilled out of my palms as I nuzzled her neck, seeking out my favorite spot, just behind her ear. Her thready pulse jumped under my lips, and I wanted to make her feel like this forever. I inhaled deeply before tracing my thumbs over her nipples. Groaning low, Neela locked her legs around my waist and cried out.

The words slid off my tongue in a whimper. "Darling, you are so goddamned beautiful." Her scent completely intoxicated me, making me shake. "I can't get you out of my head."

When she dug her hands into my hair, I growled against her throat.

Control, I needed to find some goddamned control. All I had to do was relax a little. *Don't rush.* But fuck, I wanted to rush. She was rubbing her body against mine, writhing in my arms, and I wanted to do lots of other things to elicit that reaction.

Neela arched her back and the last tenuous hold I had on my control evaporated.

Picking her up easily, I blindly marched us upstairs and into the bedroom before I deposited her in the middle of the bed without breaking the kiss. Well aware of how much smaller she was, I was careful not to lay my whole weight over her. Instead, I shifted us to our sides and settled her against me fully. With a rough groan, I hiked up a handful of her skirt, exposing her flesh to my hands.

"Fuuuuck."

The tingling in my spine spread quickly and the thundering roar of my heartbeat drowned out any other sound but her moans, mewls and little gasps.

Frustration riding me, I shifted our bodies again so I could yank my shirt over my head before settling myself back against her. My cock aligned against the hot center of her body and I bit back a moan when Neela lifted her hips into mine.

I dropped my forehead to hers, breaking the kiss, then gnashed my teeth together while I tried to quiet the tornado of emotions. With a feather-soft touch, she cupped my cheek and kissed me softly. There was something so tender, unguarded, and vulnerable about her in that moment, and I was lost. Her soft touch was enough to force honesty out of me.

"What are you doing to me? I am so desperate to be inside of you right now."

Her fingers drifted down my face, over my collarbone. And I held my breath as she grazed my nipple. It made her smile. Sliding lower, she traced each of my abs as if counting them. But it wasn't until she traced her fingers over my happy trail that I started to shake. Shit, I had to get myself under control.

I released her and in record time shed my belt, leaving my pants hanging low on my hips. I didn't want to rush this. I didn't want to lose the way this felt. Didn't want it to evaporate.

When I slid back into bed, I gripped her hips reflexively as I kissed her again, rolling my hips into hers. The only sounds permeating the room were our gasps and groans as I devoured her with my mouth. From the way my skin hummed everywhere she touched me, I knew sliding into her would be heaven. I knew we would be combustible. Knew that she would own me. Because a small part of her did already.

Neela arched into my body with a satisfied groan when I captured her breast in my palm, filling my hand and then some. I teased the peak with my thumb, moaning in satisfaction when it pebbled under my touch. I wanted her crazy for me, desperate for release, desperate for connection. I wanted her to feel what I felt.

"Fuck, this has to go." With an impatient yank, I dragged her top up and shoved her skirt down. Neela fumbled with the straps and I stilled her hands. "Let me." Her hands shook as they fell away, and her gaze never left me. Deftly, I unsnapped the hooks holding the blouse together on her slim shoulders and tugged it up over her head.

She lay back and my eyes devoured every inch of her from her firm, toned legs to the lush curve of her hips, to her flat stomach with the hint of a six-pack. But my focus strayed to her full breasts and dark nipples peeking at me behind delicate lace.

I dipped my head, teasing the nipple by blowing a warm breath across the peak and her breath caught.

When I grazed the tip with my teeth, Neela laced her fingers into my hair and tugged me closer, as if willing me to take her into my mouth, to suckle her. It wasn't until I wrapped my lips around the nipple that she rocked her heated core along my cock, stroking me with the satin and lace of her panties. Teasing me with the promised heat and slickness of her pussy.

My hands coasted up her silky-smooth thigh to the elastic of the flimsy material. Shifting the fabric aside, I stroked my fingers over her slippery folds. As soon as my questing fingers tentatively dipped inside her, she raked her nails over my scalp and a harsh cry tore from her throat.

I retracted my finger then stroked her again, sliding my finger a little deeper. With each glide, I took more of her. Eventually adding another finger as my palm rubbed over her clit. I wanted her as mine. Wanted to know that *I'd* made her come. "That's it, darling, come for me, don't hold back. I want to see it. I need your pussy milking my fingers—your slickness coating them. Show me what you'll do to my cock when I fuck you."

She dragged her eyes open and blinked up at me, our gazes locking as her back bowed. She was coming—and she was fucking incredible. As if timed perfectly to hers, my body fought against the restraint I tried to apply.

Fuck. Oh God. Blinding light danced on the edges of my vision. As quivers wracked her body and her pussy pulsed around my fingers like they were my cock, I felt pleasure with the force of a tsunami chasing up my spine. *No. No, no, no.*

Not now, not like this. I wanted to be *inside* her.

With a low growl, I shifted her so that she lay flat on her back against the pillows and I lay next to her, still nuzzling her neck. Slowly, I slid a hand over her stomach, up and over her ribcage again to gently palm her breast.

My gaze dropped to her lips as I said, "I wonder if you can come just from me touching your breasts. You think you'll like it if I take that pretty nipple into my mouth?"

She squirmed underneath me. "Jax, please."

"Maybe there's somewhere else you want me to touch? Somewhere else I can make you feel good?"

She raised her hips giving me a direct hint. My chuckle was low. "I'll get there, I promise. Since I only get one shot at this, I'm going to take my time."

"Yes, please."

I dropped my head and took a nipple into my mouth as Neela arched her back. As I sucked her deep, my thumb teased the other nipple, and I laved at her, teasing her with my teeth and tongue, worshiping her.

I released her breast and skimmed a hand down her torso and past her belly. Neela threaded her fingers into my hair and I shifted her legs wider to give me access. Lifting my head from her breast, I watched her intently as I slid a finger inside her. "My God, you are so fucking wet." With a shiver rolling through her, Neela let her lids flutter closed as I coaxed a response out of her. "No, sweetheart. I like you to look at me."

Neela forced her lids open even as her body started to quake. With my eyes and my body and my fingers, I demanded she be present right there with me. There was no hiding her response. No hiding what I did to her. No hiding that she needed it.

The fingers on my other hand busied themselves by penetrating her slow and steady with a measured retreat. Only to dip back inside her, stretching her. I refused to break eye contact with her. Refused to let her hide from what I was doing to her. I insisted that she be vulnerable and gave her no less in return.

Finally, I captured her wrists in one hand and pinned them above her head. With my other, I yanked out my wallet and pulled out a condom. With quick efficiency, I had myself sheathed and lay poised between her thighs.

Through gritted teeth, I asked, "Are you sure?"

Instead of words, she arched her hips, inviting me in. I parted her thighs and rubbed the head of my cock against her slick heat. "Fuck, you're so ready."

Neela's hands traced my back and shoulders, loving how the muscles bunched under her hands.

I pressed inside and groaned as she took me deep. She hissed at the size of me, but more from pleasure than pain. I dropped my forehead to hers and with a slow, torturous retreat, slid back until I was almost out of her. When I drove back in, the hint of bite was gone and all that remained was the fierce, tingling pleasure.

I took my time. I wanted to savor every moment, even as the sweat slicked both our bodies and she begged me, I continued the pace. The only time I changed my thrusts was when I kissed her long and deep, as if we were fused at the lips. Only our shallow breathing and soft moans of, "So soft... God, yes..." and "Right there..." permeated the silence.

Abruptly, my back stiffened and my brows snapped down. Leaning forward and kissing her again, sliding my tongue over her as I licked into her mouth, I also smoothed my thumb over her clit. Expertly, knowing just how she liked it, just what she'd need to fly. And I pushed that button.

My name was a scream on her lips, but her calls were drowned out by my own. The lightning raced up my spine, exploding through my body and I held her locked in place as we consumed each other in bliss.

Chapter twenty-one

JAX

I shouldn't be kissing her, but it's not like I gave a shit about that now. I'd spent the early hours of the morning shagging the most beautiful woman on earth. Okay not shagging to be precise, I'd woken her up with my tongue on her clit.

Sue me, I was hungry. And she was just the flavor I wanted. I could do nothing else but watch Neela come for the rest of my life, and I'd be okay with that.

God I was such a fucking addict. I couldn't stop touching her.

Ariel was waiting outside the gate at the bottom of the hill. She couldn't see us kissing. And Mayzie was in her car seat, currently eating her toes and completely distracted.

"Come here."

Neela giggled and tried to slip my grasp, but I was too quick. "Jax, I want to keep this under wraps for now."

"And I absolutely agree. But I'm going to need a kiss first."

She giggled again. And I loved that sound. When I met her she was too serious, too scared. Too... something.

As my lips splayed over hers, all the blood went straight to my dick.

Down boy.

Fat lot of good that did. He only got harder. Just smelling her was enough right now. It didn't matter that I had spent the better half of the last twelve hours basically locked inside her, I couldn't let go.

This is so dangerous and stupid.

I didn't care, though. I wanted her. And now that I'd had her, letting go was going to be a problem.

She drew back slightly even as her arm looped around my neck. "What are we going to do with you?"

"The question is what are we going to do with you? We could go back inside. Put Mayzie in a playpen..."

"No. Take her to the park, please. I have to get to work. I do have to run my company. Adam needs me. Bex has calls waiting for me. I need to go."

I groaned low. "Why?"

"You know why."

"Yeah I know. It's just, I keep thinking about this morning and how your nails felt digging into my skin."

There was a slight flush under her skin, making her cheeks slightly darker. "Stop."

"No need to blush. I liked it."

She giggled again and tucked in. "Oh my God, this is so insane."

I kissed her forehead. "Stop. It feels good. You like it, right?"

"Yeah, I like it too much. But you're here for Mayzie, not for me."

"I'm here for the both of you as long as you need me."

I bit my tongue before I said anything else stupid. I wanted her to need me. I wanted her to want me around. But I could tell she was skittish, so I wasn't going to say that. "Just enjoy what's happening, okay?"

She bit her bottom lip and nodded. "Okay."

"All right, let me get her out of here before I really do throw you back inside, or worse in the car."

"Mayzie's in there."

"I know. But her car seat is facing the back. I just, God, I can't stop touching you."

"I know. I like how it feels. And I feel… I don't know, crazy, desperate, and a little out of control."

"Yeah it's a rush. It's like a high. I've been thinking about how you would taste since the moment I saw you. And now that I know, I'm like an addict. I can't stop."

"We have to stop. You take Mayzie. I need to get to work."

"Okay. Just be careful."

I released her. I had to. But on the cellular level, my body rejected that idea. My hands twitched on her hip trying to hold her to me. But I knew what I had to do. When she wiggled out of my grasp I skipped up the sidewalk to the landing in front of the house. I went around to the driver's side of the car and climbed in. I checked quickly on Mayzie, who was still eating her toes, slobbering all over them in fact. "Alright, love? Ready to go to the park?"

Her response was a slobber. And then she clapped and reached for something.

Shit. The damn bunny. I opened the door and climbed out. Neela had already turned, but she whirled back around. "More kisses?"

"As much as I would love that, we forgot Bunbun."

"You stay. I'll get it."

"No. I need to chase it down. I think it's maybe in her room? Or the living room."

"You stay with Mayzie. I'll be right back."

I watched her run into the house. I eased back into the driver's seat. "Mayzie, you think I cocked it all up?"

She made a motoring sound.

"You're right. I can't mess this up. I can keep both of you safe, I swear."

More blubbering.

"You know Mayzie, I like you kid. You make it really easy to talk to you."

She clapped her hands and then said "Sa sa."

I groaned. But still, I slipped into the verse of "I Can't Get No Satisfaction."

I needed to tread carefully. Because if I wanted to hold onto Neela and Mayzie after all this was over, I couldn't fuck this up. I needed to find a way to keep them.

I needed to find a way to tell her the truth.

NEELA

Okay, if I were a stuffed bunny where would I be?

I checked the living room and the kitchen first. Mayzie had been playing there in the morning, and she was never really without that toy.

My phone rang in my pocket, and I pulled it out.

"Hey, boss lady, you've had three calls this morning. You coming in?"

"Sorry, Bex. I'm trying to find Mayzie's toy. I'll be there soon as I'm done, okay?"

"Sure thing. I just wanted to check since I know you wanted to head over to the gallery today."

"Yep, I'm on it, I swear."

There was a beat. "You okay? You sound, I don't know, weird."

Weird didn't even begin to cover it. "Yep, great. I'll see you soon."

I hung up without giving her a chance to ask any more questions. I knew what she would say. She would pounce on this. And honestly, I didn't know what the hell was going to happen. Or what *was* happening. I knew we couldn't seem to keep our hands off of each other. The moment he'd touched me, it had been like fire to a match. I'd never felt like that in my life.

And then, well, this morning. I'd never done anything like that. If I was being honest, Richard wasn't much for snuggling or lazy lie-ins. Not that the morning had been a lie-in, because we woke up at half-past six. But Richard didn't like morning sex. There were a lot of things Richard didn't like that I accommodated, and I realized that I had been catering to Richard's viewpoint of me not being sexy or adventurous enough. Apparently, I was plenty adventurous.

Careful. You will fall for this guy.

I couldn't fall for him. He worked for me. I'd already made that mistake once. I didn't want to make it again.

But I knew instinctively that Jax and Richard were different people. Richard was one kind of man, and Jax was a complete other. That still didn't mean that any of this was a good idea, but I couldn't stop myself. Because if I was being honest, I would have taken him up on that whole shag-in-the-front-seat thing.

What was wrong with me?

It's been a while since you've had some orgasms.

Okay, yeah, so that's what was wrong with me. I mean, I could run down there, bring Mayzie her toy, put her in her playpen, and just get one more orgasm from the man.

You're an addict.

I was totally an addict.

Just like that, I was addicted to having sex with him. To having him inside me. To the way his eyes pierced mine and his quiet commands. Watch me. Touch me. Bite me.

I shivered. No. Focus. Find the damn toy.

It wasn't in the kitchen or the living room. I took the stairs two at a time and ran to the bathroom and then to Mayzie's room. No luck. On my way back downstairs to do another sweep of the living room, I saw something fuzzy on the corner of Jax's nightstand. I paused. Oh, there it was. Maybe he'd been carrying it this morning for some reason and forgot it.

I jogged in and scooped it up off the corner of the nightstand. My gaze flickered downward to the drawer that was partially open.

What the hell? There was something black and metallic inside.

I knew better. I absolutely knew better, but I still couldn't stop myself. What in the hell—

I pulled the drawer open.

The bottom fell out of my stomach. I didn't know much, but I certainly knew what a gun magazine looked like. I'd seen enough action movies. That's exactly what that was. And maybe Willa had it from before. But where was the gun? Where the hell was the gun safe? And why the hell did my fucking nanny have a gun magazine?

I grabbed it along with the toy. A cold numbness started from my toes and wound its way up, swirling, cutting off all circulation, all feeling, all sensation as it wound around my ankles, my calves, my thighs, worming its way up to my core. Chilling me to the bone. And then finally it flooded my arms to the fingertips. I could feel nothing.

I jogged out the front door, and Jax was grinning at me as he climbed out of the car. "Where'd you find it?"

I handed him Mr. Ta. "Your bedroom. Along with this." I placed the magazine in his palm, and then I met his gaze.

"Shit, Neela—"

"You're not a manny, are you?"

To be continued in...Tempting the Heiress!

Looking for a few Good Books? Look no Further

FREE

Sexy in Stilettos

Game Set Match

Bryce

Shameless

Before Sin

Royals

Royals Undercover

Cheeky Royal

Cheeky King

Royals Undone

Royal Bastard

Bastard Prince

Royals United

Royal Tease

Teasing the Princess

Royal Elite

Accidental Heiress

Royal Protection

The Bodyguard Dilemma

The Donovans Series

Come Home Again (Nate & Delilah)

Love Reality (Ryan & Mia)

Race For Love (Derek & Kisima)

Love in Plain Sight (Dylan and Serafina)

Eye of the Beholder – (Logan & Jezzie)

Love Struck (Zephyr & Malia)

London Billionaires Standalones

Mr. Trouble (Jarred & Kinsley)

Mr. Big (Zach & Emma)

Mr. Dirty(Nathan & Sophie)

The Shameless World

Shameless

Shameless

Shameful

Unashamed

Force

Enforce

Deep

Deeper

Before Sin

Sin

Sinful

Brazen

Still Brazen

The Player
Bryce
Dax
Echo
Fox
Ransom
Gage

The In Stilettos Series
Sexy in Stilettos (Alec & Jaya)
Sultry in Stilettos (Beckett & Ricca)
Sassy in Stilettos (Caleb & Micha)
Strollers & Stilettos (Alec & Jaya & Alexa)
Seductive in Stilettos (Shane & Tristia)
Stunning in Stilettos (Bryan & Kyra)

~ ~ ~

In Stilettos Spin off
Tempting in Stilettos (Serena & Tyson)
Teasing in Stilettos (Cara & Tate)
Tantalizing in Stilettos (Jaggar & Griffin)

The Chase Brothers Series
London Bound (Alexi & Abbie)
London Calling (Xander & Imani)

Love Match Series
*Game Set Match (Jason & Izzy)
Mismatch (Eli & Jessica)

About the
author

USA Today Best Seller, Nana Malone's love of all things romance and adventure started with a tattered romantic suspense she "borrowed" from her cousin. It was a sultry summer afternoon in Ghana, and Nana was a precocious thirteen. She's been in love with kick butt heroines ever since. With her overactive imagination, and channeling her inner Buffy, it was only a matter a time before she started creating her own characters.

Now she writes about sexy royals and smokin' hot bodyguards when she's not hiding her tiara from Kidlet, chasing a puppy who refuses to shake without a treat, or begging her husband to listen to her latest hairbrained idea.

Printed in Poland
by Amazon Fulfillment
Poland Sp. z o.o., Wrocław